On leaving school, I trained to be an electrician, and once qualified, I became a professional manager becoming a member of the institute of managers. I retired on health grounds in 2006, I then developed an insatiable thirst for knowledge, which inspired me to train as a freelance journalist and become an author and during my research into stroke recovery, I uncovered what I believe to be a conspiracy by government to prevent people living with disabilities from becoming able bodied once more.

I lost my wife when she was only forty-eight, after she suffered a major stroke, I myself suffered a stroke when I was 52 years of age and I have been left with a disability.

Dedication

I dedicate this book to my late wife Colette, the best thing that happened to me in the whole of my life and who was also the biggest influence on my life. Even though we didn't have enough time together, the time we did have with each other, each and every second was precious. There were lots of things we planned to do that we never managed to do and it breaks my heart knowing what we have missed out on, however I still have so many fantastic memories of our time together, memories that will never fade and while I can no longer see you, I firmly believe you are still with me the whole of the time and you are still a large influence in my life today. I don't think I told you as often as I should how much you meant to me, or told you as often as I should how much I loved you, although I'm sure you knew just how much you did mean to me.
In the words of your favourite singer
YOU'RE IN MY HEART YOU'RE IN MY SOUL.
You provided me with the most fabulous gift you could have. Our Daughter Catherine, I'm sure you would be so proud of her by what she's achieved and also by her choice of boyfriend, I know that I am. I still love you with every part of my body. RIP my darling and I hope we will be together again one day.
I would like to pay thanks to all my family, my friends and my in laws for all their help, support and the strength they have given me during these difficult last ten years and for also listening to my ramblings about this book during the time I have been writing it and for their patience and understanding.
Love you and God bless you all.
Extra special thanks go to my Daughter Catherine and her partner Adam, without their help and understanding I couldn't have survived and to my brother Peter who is also my best

friend, his wife my sister in law Mavis, not to forget my nephew Paul, you're a star, mate, nothing is ever too much trouble to you and you bring a smile to everyone who meets you.

Thanks to everyone and apologies to anybody I have failed to mention.

Steven Thomas-Leah

DECEPTION

Copyright © Steven Thomas-Leah (2015)

The right of Steven Thomas-Leah to be identified as author of this work has been asserted by him in accordance with section 77 and 78 of the Copyright, Designs and Patents Act 1988.

All rights reserved. No part of this publication may be reproduced, stored in a retrieval system, or transmitted in any form or by any means, electronic, mechanical, photocopying, recording, or otherwise, without the prior permission of the publishers.

Any person who commits any unauthorized act in relation to this publication may be liable to criminal prosecution and civil claims for damages.

A CIP catalogue record for this title is available from the British Library.

ISBN 978 1 78554 886 4 (Paperback)
ISBN 978 1 78554 887 1 (Hardback)
ISBN 978 1 78554 888 8 (E-Book)

www.austinmacauley.com

First Published (2016)
Austin Macauley Publishers Ltd.
25 Canada Square
Canary Wharf
London
E14 5LQ

Colette was my inspiration behind this book, so, my darling, this one's for you.

I can't finish this part of my book without mentioning my late Mother Alma who recently passed away; thanks, mam, we all owe and miss you so much.

Contents

The First Meeting	6
The Cat's Out of the Bag	30
Matthew and his Big Mouth	52
Don't Insult my Intelligence	63
Downing Street	88
Back in Manchester	114
The Best Taxi Ride Ever	135
The Compromise Agreement	140
The Independent Hearing	147
The Judicial Enquiry	154
The Conclusion	172
The Press Release	183
Ironic or What	193
Cometh the Wrong Decision Cometh the Dictator	205
Let's Get this Show on the Road	217
Back on the Island	219
It's Good News Week	222

Prologue

Every living thing will eventually die. Even the most nurtured plant in your garden will eventually die, however the keen gardener will do everything they can to keep it alive for as long as possible.

It's a disgrace that the same cannot be said about various medical authorities and governments.

In spite of how privileged our parents may be, in theory we are all born equal. Sadly we are not always treated equally throughout our lives and some of us die far too young unnecessarily. Just take the health post code lottery as an example, I may live in ABC 123 and be denied essential treatment to help treat a condition I'm suffering from, treatment which could help prolong my life and maybe even give me my life back, my neighbour however who lives across the road in BCD 456 and suffering the same ailment, is able to receive the essential treatment to help cure them, why? It's usually down to money. I pay the same taxes, yet I'm the one who dies.

Why?

Following my wife's premature death and my own illness, I started to ask these and many other questions. I remembered being told way back in the 1970s and 80s that the next medical breakthrough would be stem cell treatment, so where is it?

Why are we not reaping the benefits from this new treatment? I have spoken to countless specialists during the last ten years. I have enquired about the possibility of stem cell treatment aiding my own recovery, only to be showered with countless negatives about this treatment, it's as if these medical experts didn't want to, or were being prevented from talking about this treatment. One neurologist even replied yes he believed this treatment would eventually be adopted and help cure many ailments *but not in my life time*!

So I ask this question. Why not in my life time?

Stem cells do not have to be invented they are with us today; every one of us contains them. So why can we not use them today?

I know countless numbers of people who are stroke survivors and people who have been born with a brain disorder but I know of no one who has been offered stem cell treatment!

I have carried out a great deal of research into stem cell treatment and have found that this treatment is available and being used successfully in countless countries throughout the world but only in private clinics, however it is a very expensive procedure because the patient has to pay for the treatment themselves, plus the associated costs, flights, accommodation, etc. Sometimes even as much as fifty thousand dollars, I know this sounds a lot of money but what price do you put on good health, if this treatment was adopted and was available on the NHS the cost of providing this treatment would be a fraction of what private patients currently have to pay.

I have read countless anecdotal reports about the success of this treatment in aiding various debilitating conditions.

I have asked this question of myself, are these clinics targeting vulnerable people as a means of making money and is it just a scam?

This is something I can't answer. Is this treatment genuine? This is another question I can't answer.

I do, however, eventually intend to have an answer, either by recovering myself after receiving this treatment, or exposing these people for what they really are.

The story of corruption in this book is purely fictitious and a figment of my own imagination, however owing to the amount of research I have carried out into this treatment, I personally believe there is some truth in the claims that stem cell treatment is a viable option to aid in the treatment of some serious illnesses.

In writing this book, I am hoping that I may inspire the reader to ask question's themselves of their own medical contacts and hopefully at least open some form of debate about stem cell treatment and uncover the truth one way or another about this treatment, can it be relied on and if it can why is it not available to us today?

From Christopher Columbus through to Neil Armstrong, man has always had a desire to explore new territory and understand everything about it. It's echo culture, how it works, etc. We are, however, running out of new things and places to explore and understand. There is, however, one place on earth that still holds the mystique, that previous explorers have found irresistible and that place is the brain, how it works, how do we fix it when it goes wrong? Sadly it appears that successive governments in both the UK and US have given up on that expedition. However billions of dollars are spent each year exploring the cosmos, in search of little green men. If we were to spend this colossal amount of money on medical research, maybe we would already know these answers.

Thankfully there are still a number of pioneers out there who continue to explore this remarkable organ. Pioneering scientists and doctors, who refuse to be tethered by conventional medical theories and so called ethics. In recent times it has been acceptable to grow a beef burger from stem cells at a cost in excess of £200,000. Tell me if you can where are the ethics behind this experiment?

What if the same £200,000 had been spent on medical research into the use of stem cells in tackling illness?

As I have already mentioned most of this novel is fictitious but could I have hit on something? Why are stem cells not used today by the medical authorities in the UK or sanctioned by the Government? Do people have too much to lose if they were?

I will leave you to Judge for yourselves.

I remember reading somewhere, that in 2013, US President Barak Obama announced that the USA was going to spend whatever it takes to understand how the brain works.

Too little too late for too many people I may add!

While I am no medical expert, nor am I an authority in any form of medical treatment, neither am I a gullible person. I have an inquisitive mind and ask questions. So let me ask this final question of you and the medical experts. Why is it, that anyone including myself can discover details about stem cell treatment which appears to provide hope in aiding in the recovery of so many different ailments, ailments such as my own, ailments according to these private clinics which include some forms of blindness, different forms of paralysis, in addition to stroke and even Alzheimer's, don't take my word for it. Just type into any search engine, progress with stem cell treatment and discover many of these clinics worldwide. If these claims are bogus, why doesn't the government and medical authorities advise us against being taken in by them?

They are all too eager to prevent us our right to smoke wherever and whenever we want too, or telling us how much alcohol we should drink, or arguing between themselves about should we or should we not be in the EEC and how people are claiming too many state hand outs and even how we should spend the money most of us are entitled to claim in the first place. Personally as a disabled person and I think I can speak for most people living with a disability, I would prefer to not be in a position where I have to rely on these benefits. I would much prefer to be able to work and earn a living myself. So if stem cell treatment is a means of that happening, why am I being denied that right?

Just one last thing I would like to say, I am convinced that this treatment should be at least trialled in the UK, but what would be the effect on the pharmaceutical companies if it proved to be a success, no doubt their profits would tumble as a result of the loss of sales of all the drugs they sell to keep disabled people alive, drugs that would no longer be required, call me cynical but I'm talking about the same pharmaceutical companies who have developed a treatment that can increase the survival of some cancer patients but refuse to provide it at a price the NHS can afford therefore denying people a chance of living longer, this surely can't be right, not in my mind it can't anyway. So why doesn't the government intervene and force these companies to provide these drugs at a price we can afford? Could it be if they did they would receive less tax revenue as a result of the pharmaceuticals profits being reduced? Maybe I'm wrong, or am I?

I will leave it up to you to make up your own mind!

Chapter 1
The First Meeting

Mathew was about to embark on one of the most remarkable periods of his life. What seemed to be just a chance meeting with a stranger suddenly placed him in a situation where nothing would ever be the same again. When Matthew woke up on that morning he had no idea how the next 48 hours would change his life so dramatically. The day started just like any other day with the alarm clock waking him up.

Due to Matthew's disability he struggled to get himself out of bed and get himself dressed.

Just over six years ago, Matthew suffered a severe stroke which has left him with a slightly weakened left hand side. Matthew suffered his stroke four years after his wife died due to suffering a major stroke herself.

The difference between today and every other day since Matthews's stroke was that he was waking up in a cabin on the beach overlooking the Caribbean Sea. There was a warm but cooling breeze flowing through the cabin due to the open terrace and bed room windows. Better still Matthew had a beautiful blonde Russian lady lying by his side completely naked. You see since Matthews's stroke he had been living alone in a house near Manchester, England.

Then one day while out shopping, Matthew dropped into a bar in Manchester city centre and met this Russian beauty. He found out her name was Ekaterina, Matthew knew he was likely to forget her name, as one thing that had been affected by his stroke was his memory for names. So he decided to associate her name to something he would remember, she was studying nursing at university, which was located close to Manchester and she was based at North Manchester General hospital. They began to see each other regularly and after a short time she moved in with Matthew, to help take care of him and it also helped with her training and her course work.

Only a couple months later, here they are on holiday together in St Kitts and Nevis in the Leeward Islands. They had made plans today to go on a jeep safari around the island and visit places where tourists rarely get to see and only ten minutes after the trip began they stopped at a ramshackle bar in the middle of nowhere. For Matthew the trip was over as he noticed there were people already drinking, so he was happy at this location and didn't need to see any more of the island. The bar was surrounded by a forest of palm trees and tropical growth. They were both looking for something to eat and drink. The smell of the food attracted them like iron filings to a magnet, although the main attraction for Matthew was the beer pump on the bar and the large display of liquor bottles on the shelf behind it.

They sat in the shade of some overhead branches and where they were sitting they were almost deafened by the sound emanating from the undergrowth, the sound of crickets and other wildlife.

"I wouldn't want to have to walk into there and look for something," Matthew stated. Matthew's biggest phobia was cockroaches and other insects.

They were also being deafened by the sound from the speakers on either side of the bar. The thin black fabric fronts were vibrating due to the volume blaring out Bob Marley and Eddy Grant songs, the same ones played over and over again. Even though Matthew had never been a fan of reggae music, he couldn't help but enjoy the music, as it added to the atmosphere and the authenticity of the location. Everyone around the bar, even an old couple in their eighties if they were a day, were singing along with and swaying to the music. The old man was even wearing a Rasta hat.

Matthew and his Russian girlfriend both agreed that their first couple of drinks at this bar was probably the most enjoyable part of their holiday. They didn't exactly know why as they had previously dined by candle light in some fantastic restaurants, with breathe-taking views overlooking the sea and the fabulous coastlines of the island. Restaurants in which they had consumed some of the most exotic food either of them had ever eaten, yet they found themselves sitting in what can only be described as a jungle, fighting off mosquitoes and eating fried chicken, using their fingers. They were sitting on plain patio furniture in tropical temperatures. There was no air conditioning in this wooden ramshackle shack and there was what can only be described as a garden shed used for a rest room and shared by both genders. The shed had a lone cold water tap on the outside for you to wash your hands on your way out. Matthew was imagining a situation most people have experienced. Maybe not quite like this location but a state of mind, where we may have had the very basic of amenities but we still can't explain why we had such a good time and we all have such fond memories of.

Matthew has spent a considerable amount of time at a location closer to home in Tenerife at a bar that has nothing to offer. You can't buy food, there is no entertainment and it is situated on a dusty main road and owned by a grumpy old Spaniard. However whenever Matthew would go to this resort on holiday, it is the first place he would head for. Matthew usually went on holiday with his Brother Jim, Jim's wife, Betty and their son and Matthew's favourite nephew Andy.

Betty when asked where in the world she would prefer to be at any given moment in time, you could bet your bottom Dollar that this bar is where she would choose. Just as Matthew will always have fond memories of this brief moment in time as his favourite part of this holiday.

Then something happened that on reflection changed the mood in the bar somewhat and Matthew's life dramatically. They both sat there sipping cocktails and eating fried chicken. Matthew commented he had never tasted anything like it before and then from the speakers for at least the tenth time, the same Bob Marley song came on. ***Don't worry about a thing because every little things going to be alright.***

Matthew thought to himself about the irony of this particular song. *At this moment in time with drink in hand, cigarette lit in the ash tray, fantastic finger food on tap, unique surroundings and a beautiful Russian lady, who he knew he would be sleeping with that night and not just sleeping with he hoped,* if you get his drift, Matthew didn't have a worry in the world. That would come later on.

Suddenly from the undergrowth appeared a little emaciated scruffy brown mongrel dog, which started running around their feet looking for any scraps that may be going. The poor little thing was so thin you could have played music on its ribs. It was also showing signs of having had pups, as its teats were sagging under its body and were completely devoid of milk. Everyone in the bar was enthralled by this cute little animal and were looking over at Matthew and his friend.

Matthew, being a dog lover and feeling like another drink as well, stood up using the corner of the table to assist him to stand. He picked up his walking stick to help with his balance and walked to the counter, where he ordered two more cocktails. This time he ordered himself a Manhattan and a Mojito for his friend, as well as some more deep fried chicken which he intended to feed to the dog. When he turned around to look for his friend, to ask her if she would be kind enough carry the tray back to the table, Matthew noticed their starving little friend had been joined by another six little dogs, each one a clone of the first one and each of them fighting one another to get to the larger dog trying to suckle from it.

These pups were obviously her litter, so Matthew turned to the guy behind the bar and asked for a bowl of water, a bowl of milk, and another three portions of chicken. The pack were now sitting together underneath Matthew's table, eagerly awaiting his return with this delicious smelling cooked chicken, suddenly the pack became restless and began running around all the other tables, all of them yapping trying to gain attention and food from the other customers. The dogs were all enjoying being petted and the attention they were receiving but they were still keeping their attention firmly fixed on Matthew. When the food was ready Matthew's friend walked up to the counter where she collected the tray and carried the first order of chicken to the table, the dogs returned to Matthew's table and started to go wild with excitement. Ekaterina striped the meat off the bone and dropped it one piece at a time on the floor. The greedy Alpha pup was barking and snapping at the other pups, fighting with each one of them in an attempt to pinch their food. Suddenly the Mother took control and chased the bully away and being the good mother she was she made sure the rest of the litter could get their fair share. After she ensured each pup had, had at least had a mouthful, she decided it was now time to get her share. While Matthew was waiting for his latest order of chicken he ordered himself another Manhattan and another Mojito for Ekaterina. Matthew was now getting tired and he needed a chair to sit down. He asked a couple who were sat close by if they would mind if he sat on one of their spare chairs.

A lone customer caught Matthew's attention and offered him one of his spare chairs. They introduced themselves to each other, the stranger was called Mark.

"Would you prefer if I fetched the chair to the bar for you? Or would you like to join me at the table?" Mark asked.

Matthew agreed to join him and walked over to the table but before doing so he turned to ask his Russian beauty to join him, she declined the offer for now and continued to sit where she was, taking a magazine from her bag, relishing this brief moment in time to catch up on some celebrity gossip in this latest version of Cosmopolitan magazine, she had become obsessed with this type of magazine, since she had moved to the west, as it was something she couldn't get her hands on back in her native country. Even though she hadn't lived in England that long, she was even surprised herself at just how quickly she had become westernised. Russia even though it hadn't been a year since she lived there, was now just a distant memory. Matthew repositioned the chair so it was easier for him to sit down and face the stranger. Mark spoke with a soft American accent. He offered to buy Matthew a drink and as it would be rude to refuse, Matthew accepted his offer.

"Would you mind if I have a Manhattan?" Matthew asked.

"No not at all. In fact I think I will join you in one of those."

Mark called the waiter over and placed the order for the drinks but rather than order two Manhattans Mark ordered a full jug, or as Matthew now knows it, a pitcher. ***This is my kind of drinking buddy*** Matthew thought to himself. They sat there in these idyllic surroundings chatting as if they had known each other for years. Mark began telling Matthew all about his life while he was growing up in New Jersey USA, which was a lot more interesting than Matthew's own upbringing in New Moston Manchester, England. None the less, it was a very enjoyable conversation. Mark described in very eloquent detail how he used to visit little Italy in New York. He shared a memory of one night while having a meal in Little Italy, he explained how he found himself sitting at the very next table to and overhearing a conversation between a small Italian-looking guy and John Gotti, the dapper, Teflon Don and New York Mafia boss. Matthew was fascinated by his story. He told Mark of his own association with the Quality Street gang, it didn't seem to have the same impact on Mark. Matthew explained who these people were and that this gang of crooks were known locally as the Manchester Mafia. Mark possessed a blank expression.

"Have you ever heard of the Krays?" Matthew asked.

"Weren't they the psychopathic twins from London who ruled the underworld in your country?"

"They thought they did until they came to Manchester and tried to take control of the city. They were sent packing by Manchester's very own Quality Street Gang, without them the Krays ever getting off the station complex, these people were no ordinary gang of crooks, not many people messed with them."

Mark seemed a little more impressed now by Matthew's association with Manchester's very own Mafia. Matthew was enjoying his time chatting with Mark.

Mark enquired, "Why were they called the quality street gang? As it seemed quite disrespectful."

Matthew's explanation was.

"I believe that one evening in a city centre pub, which was a regular meeting place for many of Manchester's underworld and while most of it was having a drink there, the Manchester mafia walked into the bar, all of them dressed in the same style grey suits, one of the crooks who was drinking in the bar that night commented, you look like the people on the top of a tin of Quality Street. It was rumoured that the person who made the comment was never seen drinking in that pub again." Matthew didn't know if this was true or just folklore, however the name stuck.

He told Mark that he had an interest in anything to do with the Mafia. Secretly Matthew had always thought he would have loved to have been born in the 1920s and been part of the Mafia of that time, maybe even part of the Capone gang.

He told Mark a lovely little story of a holiday in the 1990s in Florida with his wife and daughter, when he paid to visit a theatre called Capone's. You couldn't buy tickets you had to pay by card over the phone. You were given a password to enter the theatre. Matthew would always remember the password; it was three Cherry Coke's. The theatre was a plain looking building on the 192 highway, it had a plain wooden door with a sliding panel at eye level. Once a customer knocked on the door, the panel was opened and the customer was asked to give their pass word and they had they were allowed to enter. Once inside they were in a mock-up of a speakeasy, all the men were dressed as Gangsters and the waitresses as Gangster's molls. The entertainment was a re-enactment of the St Valentine's Day massacre, acted out on stage in a musical format. During the show for authenticity, all alcoholic drinks were served in plain white porcelain cups. To signal the end of the show the theatre was raided by uniformed cops and the FBI, who placed all the customers under arrest, their details were taken and they were read their rights. Then they were escorted out of the theatre by these cops. It was an amazing experience.

By this time Matthew's Russian beauty was becoming restless. She joined the pair of them at the table and reminded Matthew that their jeep was picking them up in 15 minutes. Mark offered to give them a ride back to their cabin as he only lived down the beach from where they were staying.

He told them he had lived on the island for the last 10 years, however not saying why, or what he had been doing here during this time.

Mark's car was parked just across the road from the bar and when the jeep turned up Matthew walked over and told the driver that they were making their own way back. Matthew quickly re-joined his friends at the table, where he found another Manhattan placed in front of where he had been sitting. They continued chatting for another couple of hours, buying a few more rounds of drinks and with each round they ordered another portion of fried chicken for their new found litter of friends. Matthew stripped the chicken from the bone; he let it cool for a while. After a couple more Manhattans the chicken was cool enough to feed to the dogs. Matthew whistled and they all ran up to the table with their tails wagging behind them. Matthew fed each one individually, making sure the bully let each one have a fair share.

Matthew called over the waiter and asked him, "Could you bring over two bowls of cold water and two of cold milk please?"

The waiter replied, "Would you like a pitcher of Manhattans with them?"

"Why not and one of Mojito for the lady please."

The waiter was not going to pass up on the opportunity to take money out of the hands of these, what seemed to him, wealthy people.

By the time they were ready to leave the bar, each one of their little friends were lying flat out in the sun and panting in unison. Their little bellies full and moving up and down with every breath they took. Matthew thought that they probably had full bellies for the first time in months.

Before they left, Matthew insisted on yet another round of drinks. After another Manhattan, Matthew attempted to stand up; he was a lot less certain on his feet than when they had arrived at the bar but certainly a lot more chilled out. They both climbed into the back of Mark's car, it was a very old American car. Mark told them it was registered in 1953. You could see from previous bumps and bangs it was a bit of a wreck. The back bumper was hanging off and all the lights were smashed, which prompted both Matthew and his Russian friend to look at one another with dread in their eyes. However they chose to be courageous and stayed in the car. The engine started with a whirling and a grinding sound as though it hadn't tasted oil since the 1950s. Then at last, on the fourth time of asking the engine started. You wouldn't say it roared into life, it was more of a whimper than a roar.

During their ten minute journey home, Matthew couldn't make out if he was in the USA or the UK as their chauffer didn't seem to care which side of the road he was driving on. It was at this point that the two of them questioned their wisdom at getting into a car with a man who was clearly not sober and fit to drive. They both kept calm at the thought that surely they will be at their destination soon enough.

At one stage of the journey they were approaching a horse and cart that was full of water melons and other tropical fruit. The workers were sat on the back of the cart. Mark over took it as if they were racing for the chequered flag in a Grand Prix. So fast that they couldn't hear the obvious abuse aimed at them by the passengers and the driver. However looking through the rear window Matthew could see how spooked the horses were and he could see the gestures being made towards them by the fruit pickers and driver. They arrived at their cabin with knuckles a lot whiter than they were in the bar. They sat in the car for a minute or two trying to get their breath back, which turned out to be a big mistake, just as they were getting out of the car the cart pulled up alongside them. The driver and workers on the cart began shouting just about every obscenity known to man. Even though Matthew could speak a little Spanish, just about enough to order a round of drinks, there were some words his Spanish tutor hadn't taught him. The workers on the back of the cart began throwing every bit of rotten fruit at them that they could lay their hands on. Matthew opened the front door and they all entered the sanctuary of the cabin. Mark insisted they join him for dinner at his home and without needing to think about it they both accepted his hospitality.

"If you don't mind we will need to shower and to change our clothes," Matthew stated.

After they had showered, both put clean clothes on. As it was still so hot, Matthew's Russian beauty opted to dress casual and put on a white bikini and a black sarong, covering her modesty at least for now anyway. Matthew took a white suit from the wardrobe he put it on the bed and asked Ekaterina to help him put it on. He realised he would probably be uncomfortable, due to how hot it was, but hoped that Mark's cabin would have some kind of cooling system installed so he decided he would have to put up with the heat, as he had no intention of sitting in the direct sunlight anyway. He put the suit on and looked in the mirror. He couldn't help but think to himself you lady killer but if the truth be known he looked more like the victim than a killer. Once they were ready, they decided that rather than risk life and limb once again by getting into Mark's car that they would walk the 100 yards or so to Mark's cabin.

When they arrived at the front door of Mark's cabin, they were greeted by a rather large, rotund black lady, the type of person whose face lights up whenever she spoke to you. She was wearing a very colourful sarong and a matching head scarf, tied in a knot at the back of her head. She led them into the very comfortable lounge of the cabin; they both thought it was breath-taking. The entire side of the cabin opened onto a veranda. On the veranda were a few wicker tables with glass tops, surrounded by wicker chairs and a matching swing which was hanging from the eaves of the veranda roof and to Matthew's relief directly above where they were sitting was a strong electric ceiling fan making the area comfortable even in these tropical temperatures. There was six reclining sun loungers placed on the white talcum powdered sandy beach in front of the veranda. The cabin was about 50 feet away from the edge of the sea. They were joined by Mark and the three of them sat, chatting and drinking even more cocktails. The cabin was surrounded by a forest of palm trees which stretched across the beach to the clear blue sea. Waves were breaking into white puffs of spray, as they washed over a small group of rocks before flowing on to the beach.

Directly in front of the cabin was a rickety wooden jetty, with a white motor launch moored alongside. It had the name Miracle painted on the bows and tied to the stern was a much smaller white speed boat called Minor Miracle.

"Who owns that motor launch and speed boat?" Matthew asked.

"I do."

Matthew thought *this guy must be worth a fortune*.

"That's a strange name for a boat. Aren't they usually named after the owner's wife or girlfriend?" Matthew enquired.

"That's right they usually are but as I had neither at the time I bought it and a short time after I purchased it something quite remarkable happened in my life."

He continued, "I decided on the name as it seemed apt."

Matthew didn't enquire what had happened, as he was now beginning to think, *this guy is either a diamond smuggler, arms dealer, drug dealer, and going by his story in the bar, maybe even a member of the Mafia.* Whatever he was, Matthew thought, *he definitely had to be something dodgy* and if he was any of these he would prefer not to know. Matthew admitted to himself at this point he was becoming a little concerned about who they had become friends with today.

After consuming even more jugs of Manhattan's, Matthew's Dutch courage and curiosity began to get the better of him. He entered into a conversation with his host about what he had been doing on the island for so long.

It turned out, rather than being involved in anything criminal Mark had been conducting medical research into stem cell treatment while on the island and Matthew discovered this was the main reason for Mark wanting to spend time with them today.

When Mark noticed them playing with the dog in the bar, it was obvious to him that Matthew was recovering from a stroke and as Matthew was a relatively young man, Mark was interested in talking to him about his condition. They discussed Matthew's life style prior to his stroke and how much it had changed following his illness. Matthew also mentioned to Mark, the death of his wife four years beforehand, following a major stroke herself and at the age of only 48. As a result of this conversation, Matthew was to learn that Mark's research was into a possible cure for his condition by using foetal stem cells. This grabbed Matthew's attention. Matthew wanted to learn more about this research and his big mouth started to operate before he engaged his brain, a trait he sometimes wished he didn't have. This was yet another occasion where he regretted what he had just said, when he did unwittingly open his mouth he never intended to embarrass or hurt the person he was talking to.

He said, "Medical research must pay well, or you're a dodgy bastard."

Thankfully Mark wasn't offended by what Matthew had said.

Matthew offered to help him with his research in any way he could, however Mark failed to reply. Mark however did refer back to his upbringing and how he had been expected to have a career in accounting and was expected to join the family business, a thriving hotel, restaurant and leisure business, which had started as just a small family run company and over a 40 year period of investment and growth, it was now a multimillion dollar listed company. At college he was expected to study business management and accounting but double entry book keeping, balance sheets, budgets and forecasts never really turned him on. His true calling was medicine. He explained how he surprised everyone by majoring in this field, specialising in neurology.

On graduating, he acquired a post graduate qualification in neurological research and was sure he could help find a cure for debilitating brain conditions. He explained how due to budget cuts his research team was disbanded and in spite of lobbying politician's country wide he was unsuccessful getting funding from anywhere, to continue with his research. He even contacted the Federal Medical Council, who invited him to present to them his progress with his research, which he was reluctant to do at first. Mark had heard rumours of researchers in the past, whose idea's had been stolen and other people had taken the credit for the discovery, however he realised he had no alternative if he was to get the funding to carry on with his dream and also have his work recognised and adopted by the medical fraternity, He described how he was devastated when the council not only rejected his research but even considered it to be too controversial to pursue. They refused to endorse it but that wasn't all, he couldn't believe it when the council barred him from carrying out his research or using his treatment anywhere in the U.S. or its tributaries. However, as he believed he was so close to making a breakthrough, he persuaded his family to provide the funds themselves for him to privately carry on with his research and he set about trying to find a location where he could carry on with his research program and if successful in finding a cure, he would be able to repay them tenfold, as his treatment would be worth billions of dollars worldwide. However money wasn't his motivation, as he had substantial personal funds of his own, owing to a legacy and an annual bond from his late father. Finding a cure was his motivation.

This was his explanation for his residence on the Island and he continued to explain how his research progressed. Which had been made possible, owing to an unexpected meeting with an old college friend and a conversation they had which had inspired him to continue with his research program. His friend had also qualified as a doctor and had decided to specialise in paediatrics. His friend had explained to him, that while working with a team of expert's, they were frantically trying to treat a poor little girl, who had developed a condition which had all the expert's mystified. They were all puzzled over how they could find a cure for her. He explained how a normal healthy child taking part in a school sport's event suddenly collapsed and was rushed to hospital. She was later diagnosed as having suffered a seizure, which had left her partially paralysed and her life in the balance. They admitted her and after initial tests placed her on life support. Her condition remained stable during the next 48 hours, so it was decided to remove her from life support but suddenly without warning she relapsed and suffered multiple seizures, one immediately after another. They placed her back on life support and carried out more blood tests, brain scans and prescribed a cocktail of the strongest and fastest acting antibiotics available. They hoped that there was some kind of infection taking place and that maybe the test results would give them a better idea of what could be causing the problem. However, the latest tests results gave them no further indication of what was wrong with her and her condition continued to deteriorate and with each seizure the damage to her brain became worse, until she became completely paralysed. In spite everything they tried, they still couldn't find out why the seizures were taking place and they had no idea how to treat her other than what they were already doing.

The team had a number of meetings with her parents and admitted to them they had no idea what to do and that their daughter was now very weak. They explained that they could offer no words of encouragement and advised the parents to prepare themselves for the worst.

Neither parent would accept this prognosis and both insisted on a second opinion, this was agreed and a team of neurological consultants from all over the world were flown in. They examined the young girl but drew the same conclusion as the first team, acknowledging that the girl's condition was something none of them had encountered before. They concluded that in her current rate of deterioration, she wouldn't last more than 12 months.

Mark thought his research was at a stage where he could offer some assistance and decided to contact the girl's parents, to discuss his research with them. He asked if they would be prepared to let him try his experimental treatment on their daughter. Through desperation, both parents willingly accepted his offer and the family flew to the island, so Mark could administer the treatment and monitor her progress over a period of time.

"What happened?" Matthew enquired eager to hear the conclusion to this tragic tale.

"You will find out in good time," replied Mark.

In the meantime while Matthew and Mark were still sitting in the shade, they could feel the temperature rising and the day getting steadily hotter. Matthew's Russian beauty couldn't resist it any longer and she moved onto the beach to soak up the sun and top up her golden tan. As she stood by one of the recliners she let the sarong fall slowly and sensuously onto the floor. Underneath her discarded sarong, was hidden an almost perfect body, or at least as close to perfect that Matthew had woken up next to in recent times. Underneath she wore the skimpiest of white bikinis imaginable, just about covering her modesty.

Without either of them saying a word, they both looked longingly at this beauty, with thoughts going through their minds only they knew, Mark picked up his Manhattan.

"You're a lucky dog, Matthew."

"I know I am," he replied.

"Right, let's have another jug of Manhattan and a smoke shall we?" Mark suggested.

Mark rang a little bell and Josie the house keeper appeared.

"Can I help you, sir?" She asked.

"Please, Josie, another pitcher of Manhattans and could you bring my cheroots oh and a pitcher of what the lady's drinking? Actually, Josie, forget the cocktails and just bring that bottle of Dom Perignon and three glasses and a jug of iced water and also could you light the barbeque and start to prepare some food for us please?"

Matthew was stunned by the very fact that along with everything else, Mark even had private waitress service. As pretentious as Matthew thought this may be, he was enjoying every minute of it.

"Are we celebrating something?" Matthew asked.

"Maybe but how about just for now, this wonderful life and our new found friendship."

"I'll drink to that."

"I don't mean to be rude, Matthew, but after spending a full day with you, I think you would drink to anything."

"You're probably right there, most things anyway."

Josie arrived with the bottle and Mark's cigarettes which he kept in a tin. There were about ten roll ups already prepared. He took one out of the tin and offered Matthew one, which he gladly accepted. He was yearning for the taste of tobacco, as he hadn't had any since they were in the bar. He held it between his fingers gently caressing it, as he would caress any part of his goddess's body, it was like he was enjoying foreplay with this dammed cigarette. He lit it and took a deeper breath than he normally would, savouring the taste of the tobacco. It tasted sweet and strange to Matthew.

He suddenly announced to Mark "I think I may have had enough to drink, as I suddenly feel light headed."

"You seem OK to me."

"Yes, I may seem OK now," he reached for his glass and poured some water into it "but my thoughts are on later this evening and the myth that has so far in my 50 something years yet to affect me but there is always a first time for everything."

Mark looked at Matthew, with a blank expression.

Matthew continued, "After the temptation which has been placed before me by my Russian beauty, I wouldn't want it to happen tonight. It's a condition known in some quarters in England, as brewer's droop, you must be aware of the effect my stroke has had on my muscles."

"Of course I am but don't worry I will help you to the car when you leave and I will even help you into your cabin, if you have a problem walking."

"That's very kind of you, but it's not the muscles in my leg that I'm afraid will be affected by alcohol, this evening."

"Oh I see what you mean." Mark sniggered and then added, "I wouldn't have thought, that would be a problem for you because if I was lucky enough to be in your position you could pickle me in alcohol, with no effect on that area. The only thing that could stop me, would be an Elephant gun fired at close range."

Mark suddenly looked embarrassed by what he had just said to Matthew.

"I'm sorry, my friend, for being so rude. A gentleman does not talk that way about a friend's lady, please forgive me."

After a few moments of silence, they both looked at each other and burst into fits of laughter.

Matthew called over to his Russian beauty and asked her to join them on the veranda. He took another long drag of his cigarette and started to feel a little faint again. He now convinced himself that he shouldn't have any more alcohol to drink. This was a very rare thought for Matthew, he couldn't remember that thought crossing his mind before. Whereas before suffering his stroke, he could drink most people under the table and he would always be the last one to go to bed, or the last to leave a party, first to arrive, last to go.

"Would you mind if I have a coffee?" Matthew asked.

Mark summoned Josie.

Josie arrived and Mark asked her to bring coffee for the three of them.

Within minutes Josie was at the table, pouring coffee, for the three of them.

Sat in this perfect location, Matthew couldn't resist asking for a brandy to accompany his coffee, this was something he and his late wife always enjoyed on their holidays, after a having meal. He knew that this wasn't the smartest idea and his new found abstinence, seemed a distant memory.

Suddenly Matthew's sense of smell kicked in. He could detect that sickly, sweet smell, associated with marijuana.

"I think that somebody is smoking dope around here," he said to Mark.

Mark laughed. "Matthew you are in the Caribbean and by the way it's not someone, it's us!"

Matthew looked at him quizzically and then at his cheroot.

"I'm a great believer, marijuana can aid in the treatment of some brain disorders" Mark added.

"Well to be honest, I would much prefer a woodbine," to explain, Matthew said "it's an old style English cigarette."

No sooner had he said that, Mark rang the bell once again. This time Josie took a bit longer to appear, but when she did she was holding another jug of ice cold Manhattans. Mark asked her if she would be good enough to fetch the 'normal cigarettes. She disappeared and brought them to the table. Even though they were not woodbines, Matthew found them much more enjoyable than the ones he had just been smoking. Matthew helped himself to a cup of coffee. He was now feeling slightly better but not yet up to another Manhattan. He asked his Russian Beauty, if she was ready to leave? Which she was. They bade their host farewell. Mark ushered another member of staff to drive them back to their cabin. Luckily Matthew had no need to be assisted.

"Can we meet for lunch tomorrow and I will show you around my research laboratory and my clinic?" requested Mark.

"Yes I will look forward to that."

"1 p.m. at your reception desk," Mark instructed.

"No problem. See you then my friend and thank you for your excellent hospitality today."

"You're welcome," came the stock American reply.

Arriving at their cabin, Matthew decided that he needed to go straight to bed, it had been a long tiring day, mainly due to the amount of alcohol he had consumed, his time in the sun and for the first time in his life, he had taken drugs. However standing in front of him was the biggest reason he wanted to go to bed, it was his beautiful Russian temptress.

Matthew's mind was going over and over his chance meeting with Mark. He was thinking about all that Mark had told him, or more to the point what he hadn't told him. However, he had more on his mind at this moment in time. To set the mood he asked his Russian beauty to sit on the veranda with him and watch the sun set.

"I could do with a coffee and a night cap before I go to bed," he added.

She agreed and made him a coffee and a brandy. Matthew had his MP3 player with him and external speakers and while waiting for his coffee, he sat on the veranda trying to find his choice of music. He made the area comfortable and he sat at the table looking out to sea and lit himself another cigarette. He programmed his MP3 player to play the music in the order he wanted. His Russian beauty appeared with a tray containing, two brandy glasses and a bottle of the best brandy Remy martin Louis XIII, or at least what Matthew considered to be the best brandy. There was a jug of white coffee and two cups he poured the coffee and two very large brandies. *What an idiot,* he thought to himself, *what about later on and the alcohol thing!* They listened to the sound of Natalie Cole, Frank Sinatra, Ella Fitzgerald, Bobby Darrin and more. Matthew was singing along to 'Mac the Knife' but sang, *Look out old Mattie is back."* Matthew's beauty laughed.

"This is wonderful, Matthew; I feel so close to you tonight," she told him.

Both of them were looking out to sea at the most fantastic sun set they had ever witnessed. It was the most romantic of settings and he had this gorgeous creature by his side.

Matthew asked, "Pass me the brandy bottle please," he lit himself another cigarette and thought to himself, *if this setting and these circumstances don't counteract the effects of alcohol, nothing will, as this must surely be nature's very own Viagra.*

He sat there, quietly thinking about the events of today and believe it or not uppermost in his mind was that pack of bloody dogs.

"Before we do anything tomorrow, I will ask the reception to make up a packed lunch."

"Oh that's nice, are you taking me on a picnic? That is one of the reasons, why I have fallen in love with you, your little spontaneous romantic gestures."

Don't ask him why as Matthew doesn't even like the taste of shoe but once again he found his size 11 foot nestled in his oversized mouth and you would have thought, by the amount of times he had tasted it he would have acquired a liking for it by now. He was putting this one down to the alcohol affecting that muscle in his skull.

"No, I want to see if on our way to the lab, Mark can go by the shack and feed the dogs."

Even before the last few words in that sentence had left his mouth, he was thinking to himself, *You asshole. All this work and expectation leading to a night of pure passion blown in one moment of muscular dysfunction.* To his surprise and delight, she burst out laughing thinking he was making a joke. Matthew never one to pass up an opportunity to make someone laugh, played along with it and now with a little bit of sanity and common sense re-entering his damaged skull muscle and no longer having the discomfort of his foot being in his mouth, he said.

"I need to get ready for bed and how about you?"

"Yes I'm getting tired myself."

"Good bring the brandy bottle will you?"

They both stood up and retired to the bedroom. He went into the bathroom to freshen up. He then went back into the bedroom and climbed into bed, his Russian beauty stood by the window with her sarong still covering her body, she then disappeared into the bathroom. He got out of bed and stood by the window, to ensure he didn't fall asleep before she returned. He was soon joined at the window by his Goddess. She was still wrapped in her sarong. He put his arm around her shoulder and softly kissed her on the cheek.

"I'm sorry but I need to get into bed," he stated.

He lay there and as his Russian beauty made her way over to the bed. He couldn't wait to get her out of her bikini and while she was walking to the bed she allowed her sarong to fall from her shoulders, he saw there was no need worrying about removing her bikini as she had already removed it in the bathroom herself. Standing before him, was a perfect specimen of a woman. While gazing at her fantastic bronzed body, he could see her only imperfections, were just two areas exposed that were milky white but rather than it looking strange, for some reason or other, it made her look even sexier. She climbed into bed and immediately started to kiss him and rub her hands tenderly over his chest, he realised in an instant, that there would be no need to use Viagra tonight.

The following morning when he woke up, Matthew showered and shaved before collecting the packed lunch from the reception desk which was situated about 30 yards from his cabin.

Chapter 2
The Cat's Out of the Bag

"Good morning," Matthew was greeted by the friendly, chatty receptionist.

"Good morning," he replied.

"Are you waiting to be picked up by Dr Cooper?"

Matthew was taken aback by this question as this was the first time he had heard Mark's surname.

"I beg your pardon, by whom?" Matthew asked. For some reason he didn't put two and two together.

The Doctor bit should have given it away but he had other things his mind this morning. Even though he had spoken to her before, for some reason this morning he found her very fancy able.

"Sorry, Matthew, I should have said the tall American gentleman you were with when you arrived back here yesterday afternoon after your jeep safari," she continued "a little worse for wear I think."

Now there is friendly and chatty, but Matthew thought rude a different trait entirely but he let her get away with it simply because he saw her in a totally different light this morning.

"You will find the doctor at the pool side bar having a coffee. Would you like me to escort you there?"

"Yes of course I would thank you."

She was a pretty young thing who Matthew had already had a drink or two with around the pool.

Matthew began thinking to himself, *Hang on in there Matt, you never know what's around the corner.* She took him by his left elbow and led him to where the doctor was. It was easy for Matthew to flirt with her.

"Good morning, Mark and how are you this morning?"

"Good morning, Matthew, I'm fine thanks just a little tired. We managed to put a fair few away yesterday you know."

"May I join you?"

"Yes, of course you may."

Matthew thanked his escort and asked her if she would be kind enough to bring him a coffee, which she did.

"What no Manhattan, Matthew?" Mark asked smiling.

"No not yet but maybe after my coffee."

"You're a beast, Matthew!"

When the receptionist returned, Matthew thanked her for everything and enquired if she would be available for a drink next time she was free.

"Yes, any time, Matthew."

"Well I will take you up on that and look forward to it."

"Are you crazy or what?" asked Mark.

"Why?"

"You're here in paradise, with one of the most beautiful women I have ever laid eyes on and you're messing about with a bit of a kid."

"Yes but a very attractive bit of a kid."

"That is not the point! You're an idiot taking the risk."

"It's always worth the risk."

Mark shook his head and swiftly changed the conversation. He asked Matthew if he could enquire about extending his stay on the island by a few weeks.

Matthew looked puzzled and asked him, "Why?"

"We need to start working together straight away."

"I'm sorry I can't I need to return on the date I planned, you see it's my daughters 21st birthday the following day."

He paused for a second before he completed what he was saying, thinking *what his wife would have said if he even considered missing it.*

"I would never be forgiven or forgive myself if I wasn't there for it."

Nowadays, before making any decision he would always think what his wife would do or say.

She always seemed to know what was best. He did miss so much about her but talking things over and making sure he did the right thing was always difficult. This however this was the type of decision everyone always referred to as a no brainer. He knew exactly what the right thing to do was.

"There is nothing that would prevent me from being there," he continued and said to Mark, "I made her an unbreakable promise that I would be home in time." He had made up his mind.

"I'm sure there must be someone else, who can help you with your research."

"Unfortunately there isn't. You see yesterday's meeting wasn't just a casual encounter. I organised it."

"I don't understand!" Matthew exclaimed.

"You see, Matthew, I had been informed about you."

"I'm sorry, informed about me by whom?" Matthew interrupted.

"By your quest of this morning."

"What do you mean my quest?"

"I mean, the young lady that you're trying to bed who works behind the reception."

"First of all, I'm not trying to bed her," *not yet anyway,* he thought to himself but carried on by saying, "I was just testing the water for now and anyway, why would she tell you about me and what could she tell you? As she doesn't know me."

"Mathew you can be a bit talkative when you're having a drink and that's what you were on your first night. You noticed a pretty face behind the reception and once you and your lady friend had settled in your cabin you came back to the bar and started talking to the young lady over a drink or two."

"Yes, that's right I did but what difference does that make?"

"Matthew, the young lady only works here part time and the rest of the time she works for me as a nurse at my clinic."

Matthew began to wonder and worry just what he had told her.

"Following your conversation, in which you told her rather a lot about yourself and the last ten years of your life, she realised you were just what I was looking for. When she spoke with me and told me about this couple who had checked into the hotel, one a beautiful Russian lady, the other a charming, relatively young Englishman, who seemed to have a health problem, I asked her to try to arrange a meeting between us and once you booked your jeep safari, she realised it was the perfect opportunity. Obviously I asked her not to tell you about me, so I could hear all about you without you telling me what you thought I wanted to hear."

"So you mean it was a set up?"

"Yes, I suppose you could call it that but not in the normal sense of the word."

"Hang on what does that mean not in the normal sense of the word, what's the difference?"

"I didn't set you up for a fall or anything like that; I just set up a meeting between us."

"Why me, and why didn't you tell me this yesterday?" Matthew was becoming more confused by the minute.

"First of all why you, just look at what you've been through. Who else do you know whose life has been affected by stroke more than yours?"

"OK, fair point, but even so."

"I said nothing yesterday because I wanted you to mill over in your mind the things I told you about my research before I could fully go into detail."

"OK, I understand what I could offer you in terms of my condition but I am confused by what the last ten years have to do with it." Matthew couldn't help but be defensive and he was becoming more frustrated by the minute.

"Matthew, while there is nothing I can do to bring your wife back, let me ask you this, how different would your life be today if your wife was still a part of it?"

"Are you joking? My life would be completely different" Matthew had a lump in his throat at this point.

"I thought so."

"Isn't that an obvious answer?"

"Yes of course it is." replied Mark. He continued, "And at the time she was ill what would you have given for her not to die?"

"Anything I could."

"Even your life?"

"Of course anything including my life."

"So what would you be prepared to give today, to stop other people going through the unnecessary pain of grief that you have?"

"I don't know at the moment but I'm sure I would be prepared to give almost anything."

"Does that also include your life?" asked Mark.

"Yes if it was a loved one of course." Matthew was utterly confused by this conversation.

"So, are you prepared to pay that price then?"

"Hey hang on now, what are you playing at, Mark?"

"I'm not playing at anything; I'm just trying to establish how passionate you are?"

"How passionate I am about what?"

"I'm talking about if you want to help me find a cure for you and people like you?"

"Of course I'm passionate about something like that."

Mark continued "That's a question everyone would answer yes to, even if I was to ask a total stranger, who was walking down the street, do you want to help me to try to find a cure for what's ailing you? From a common cold to terminal cancer the answer would be yes. It's because I wanted to know you would be open to what I'm telling you that I never mentioned any of this when we met yesterday, as I needed to get to know something about Matthew Michellin, before I knew I could have this conversation with you."

"OK but you still haven't explained what the cure is, Mark. Or what I would have to do?"

"What if I told you I could help you be as active as you were before your stroke? Due to a new treatment I have discovered."

Matthew's stomach turned and his anger grew.

"A new treatment, listen Mark I've read enough bull shit about cures like that on the internet. Some con artists claim pay us so much money and we will send you a new tablet, that will reverse your condition and cure you, or buy this new mechanical aid to help with your physical therapy and you will be amazed by what you will achieve, when at the end of the day all it is, is just a way to get vulnerable people to part with their money. These conning bastard's know how desperate some people are for a cure to their condition and that they would be willing to do or pay anything to get better and once they have parted with their money and their credit card details, they find it's a scam and no such cure exists but these bastards continue to make a fortune because there will always be someone desperate enough, to believe these scum bags who say that they're going to get better. The fact is they never do and after spending a lot of money, they find this to be nothing but a bogus claim. So I've heard all this before and I'll need a lot of convincing before I make a decision whether to help you or not."

"OK, Matthew, I understand your scepticism, it's only natural but I'm not just talking about making money and I'm not talking about a bogus cure either."

"So what are you talking about, Mark?"

"First I'm talking about absolute trust on both our parts."

"Trust, what's trust got to do with it?"

"Matthew, if I can trust you implicitly to be as committed as I need you to be and to keep my confidence and to hold you're nerve, I would like you as a partner to help me with this ground breaking discovery."

"So what do I need to trust you about?"

"You've just mentioned your doubt about these claims so I need you to trust everything I say to you."

Mark realised getting Matthew on board wasn't going to be easy and continued. "You mentioned before, Matthew, you would have been prepared to do anything, including risking your own life to have saved your wife's life."

"Yes of course I would."

"Then I asked you would you be prepared to do that for other people? You said that in theory yes you would. OK, Matthew, let me ask you a theoretical question then? When you return home, you are sadly told someone dear to you has a terminal illness. Would you then do everything you could to save their lives, including risking or giving up your own?"

"Without doubt, yes I would."

"Can I ask you this then? OK, Matthew, what would you do if I told you with your help, I could create a cure prior to your loved one becoming ill, knowing that whatever it was, it would never turn out to be terminal. Would that be enough motivation for you to do anything?"

"I'm sure it would," Matthew's anger was now receding, but his curiosity was increasing. He couldn't help but to be taken in by this intriguing thought.

"The difference is, with my wife were talking fact, she died. With this. All we're doing is talking theory."

"Well maybe not."

"Come on, Mark, stop pissing about. Is there a chance of a cure or not?"

"No there isn't a chance."

Matthew's anger returned with a vengeance. "So why are we going through all this bollocks, what the fuck do you want with me?" he demanded.

Mark's answer took Matthew totally by surprise.

"I said no there isn't a chance because that's what you asked me. Now if you had asked me can you create this cure with my help, I would have said yes I can, but you need to know that your help could place you in considerable danger and could even mean you may likely be risking your life, would you still be prepared to help me."

Matthew answered instantly, "Yes I would."

"Good! That's the answer I wanted to hear. I think I may have chosen wisely."

"Do you, Mark? That's nice to know."

Mark could sense the sarcasm in Matthew's answer.

Matthew continued, "I need to know a lot more about this."

"That's what today is all about, so we need to get going now if we're going to fit everything in."

"Hang on a minute. I'm not going anywhere, until you tell me who's going to kill me and why?"

Matthew was still not entirely convinced by Mark's story and thought, for some reason he was being had.

"Matthew, I'm not saying you're going to be killed. I am saying that it's a risk you will need to be prepared take."

"So who is it then?" Matthew asked, "Is it the Mafia?"

"I only wish it was!"

"So who is it then?" Come on, Mark, stop messing me around. Be straight with me will you but I have to say I'm glad it's not the Mafia, as I don't fancy swimming with the fishes or holding up a motorway bridge."

"If you did have to choose a way to go which way would it be?"

"I don't want to have to choose a way to go, Mark."

"Come on humour me Matthew, what would it be?"

"I'm really getting pissed off now, Mark, but if I did have to choose a way to go, how about a post coital heart attack."

"I must admit Matthew my post coital preference is a cigarette."

"So go on who will it be?"

"OK well to be honest it could be the CIA, MI5, or many other government agencies."

"Right, now I'm now getting really confused. Why, if you are claiming, you can make such a radical breakthrough of this kind, by finding a cure for all ailments as you claim you can, would government agencies be trying to silence you?"

"No, Matthew, not just claim I can, I'm claiming I have." And he continued. "They're trying to silence me simply to protect their governments. You see this treatment could have a devastating effect on financial markets worldwide."

"Go on, explain."

"Matthew all current medicines which are available for use today to try to cure most ailments would become obsolete. It's these medicines that keep the pharmaceutical companies in business."

"OK I get that."

"What do you imagine the consequences would be, of a guaranteed new cure coming on the market to these companies?"

"I would think that all their medicines would be of no use and they would probably go out of business."

It was like a light bulb had been turned on and Matthew had suddenly begun to see clearly.

"That's right! Plus most of the top doctors and top scientists would find their earning potential greatly reduced. You see these people rely on supplementing their very expensive Beverly Hills lifestyles and equally expensive Beverly Hills wives, by the research work they carry out on behalf of these companies. They get paid for trying to find new cures and products for them."

"I didn't think of that."

Mark continued "If this treatment replaced all the existing treatments and cures, where would these companies get the money from to fund new research projects? More to the point, why would there be a need to carryout anymore research into finding new treatments, or cures when we already have my miracle cure all? Hence the boat's name."

"OK, Mark, I can see that."

"Good, Matthew. There's also NASA and the Bible bashers."

"Hang on what's NASA got to do with it?" Matthew again was full of confusion and his head began to feel heavier than usual.

"America is all but broke and where has a large amount of scientific research been done in recent years?"

Matthew had a puzzled expression on his face.

"The international Space Station, that's where." Mark continued, "Also made possible with the financial backing of the pharmaceutical companies, who pay for the trips into space."

"OK, I see all of what you're saying makes sense but a breakthrough in medicine of this magnitude would be worth all those sacrifices, surely?"

"You would think it would be Matthew but if details of this was to be released it could be a massive vote loser."

"That I can't see because any government responsible for a breakthrough of this kind would certainly get my vote. I would have thought they would want to give you a Noble Prize, Mark."

Mark laughed "You would have thought so but sadly it doesn't work that way."

"Why not?"

"The simple answer to that is it was the medical, the scientific authorities and their governments, who banned this treatment from being developed."

"I don't understand, Mark."

"You see they put a stop to it being used as a cure over ten years ago; even though I knew it worked."

Mark could see that Matthew didn't fully understand, what he had just been told.

"I must say, Matthew, I'm surprised by your reaction. Did you hear what I just said?"

"Yes the government banned you using it."

"That's right I did, but I also said over ten years ago."

"OK, so you did."

"What's wrong with you, buddy, are you feeling alright?"

"Yes, fine, I'm just a bit blown away by it all."

"Matthew you still haven't realised what I've just said, have you?"

"Yes I have. You're saying that the governments banned the use of this."

"Yes, I did but I also said they banned it over ten years ago and how long ago did your wife die?"

"Oh fuck, I see what you're saying now, Mark."

"Yes!" Mark exclaimed. "I'm saying that if these bastards hadn't have banned it, your wife could still be alive today."

Suddenly Matthew had tears streaming down his cheeks.

"I'm sorry, Matthew, I didn't mean to upset you."

"I know that you didn't it's what those bastard's have done, that's upset me. I just don't believe this, Mark."

"It's true, Matthew."

"I'm not saying I don't believe you, Mark."

"Do you now see Matthew, why I just couldn't come right out and tell you this yesterday?"

"I can now but I still have a lot more questions I need to ask?"

"Go ahead."

"At what point and why did they ban this and what reason did they give you for not funding your research?"

"They banned it when I approached the Federal Medical Council for funding as I told you yesterday. First of all they ridiculed my claim. They said that I wouldn't be able to develop it and they said I had no proof just theory. Then they said and it was too dangerous and controversial to pursue and it could be financially detrimental to the US economy, clearly due to the effect on the financial markets, if the pharmaceuticals went out of business. They even said if I continued with this ridiculous claim they would strike me off the medical register and they also forbade me from carrying out research into this treatment or to try to use it anywhere in the US or any of Its tributaries. That's how I ended up here, as it's an unregulated island."

"Then what happened?"

"Do you remember the little girl, with the incurable brain condition?"

"Yes I do."

"What would you say if I told you, she now has a grown up family of her own?"

"I would say you're a liar, Mark, because if you told me the truth yesterday, you said her medical team couldn't cure her."

"That's right they couldn't but I didn't say I couldn't, did I? What I told you was that I invited her parents to bring her here for me to try and cure her."

"So did they and did you?"

"Let's get going and you'll see."

Matthew jumped up and almost ran to Mark's car, he was that keen to know the next bit of this story, all his fears of being driven by this maniac subsided.

"Where are we going?" Matthew asked.

"Were, going to my clinic."

On arrival they went straight into Mark's office. Mark inserted a video into the VCR and pressed play. Immediately a recording of a typical American family came into view, Mom, Dad and two young children in their yard. The children were playing on a swing, both of them laughing at nothing, as only children can do.

"Nice yard, Mark." said Matthew.

"No, Matthew, the little girl pushing the swing is the little girl I told you about, just two weeks before becoming ill."

He then moved the video on to an image of a little girl in a wheel chair, more disabled than anyone Matthew had ever seen in his life. So disabled that her head needed supporting by a brace to keep it from falling forward, Matthew had an image in his brain of Baron Frankenstein, her arms, legs and her body twisted in an almost grotesque fashion, her limb's twitching uncontrollably, her mouth was drooling and constantly seeping saliva. Matthew was ashamed to admit he found her hideous to look at, he noticed on the child's lap was a toy doll, the little girl couldn't remove her eyes from the doll, no doubt remembering how she once cradled it in her arms but was now unable to do so, Matthew thought he could detect the beginning of a tear stating to roll down the little girl's face. He heard Mark's voice in the background of the video.

"Sarah can you hear me and can you tell me your name please, go on try, Sarah, if you can?"

He could hear a woman's voice in the background "Come on, Sarah, sweetheart, try it for Mommy."

She tried to answer but all you could hear was an inaudible mumble and you could see just how much effort it had taken for her to perform this simple task.

"This is the child following her becoming ill," explained Mark.

"Good God why is life so cruel?" Matthew said with anger in his voice.

"I don't know but it seems that God isn't as caring as we are taught."

"A bit to theological for me that, Mark."

"Maybe it needs someone more qualified than me to try to answer your question. That is if there is anyone who can give an answer, Matthew."

"If there was it would probably be a load of bollocks anyway."

"So it's probably down to a person's faith then, Matthew."

"How can anyone have faith when you see what we've just witnessed?"

"I take it your short of faith then?"

"What little faith I had vanished ten years ago, even though being the hypocrite I am, I still pray at times like most people do."

"Not me, Matthew, I gave up praying years ago."

"Why?"

"No specific reason," replied Mark, "I think I've just witnessed too many unnecessary deaths and I had a lot of friends in the World Trade Centre on 9/11, what good, did faith do for them? Anyway let's move on, we can continue this over a drink later."

"Yes let's do that, Mark, and then we'll have a fight."

"I don't want to fight you," replied Mark.

I'll now show you a part of the video which I recorded," Mark moved the video on until he stopped at a recording of a couple around a swimming pool a man sat on a sun lounger filming the occasion and across the other side of the pool sat a lady looking fed up with the filming, as most wives do.

"Will you put that Goddamn thing away!" she shouted at the man sat on the sun lounger?"

"I just want to get a recording of the girls in the pool, then I will I promise, honey."

In the background, you could hear the sound of children tormenting each other. Suddenly two young girls came into view wearing matching costumes, both of them ran to the pool and dived in and raced each other to the other side. They climbed out and one of the little girls ran to a man who was obviously her father, he sat her on his knee, but, strangely, he seemed a lot more interested in the other little girl and never removed his gaze from her. The lady shouted to the other girl.

"Come and get dried, honey."

"OK, Mom."

It was only now that Matthew caught a glimpse of their faces.

"Mark, is that?"

"Yes it is."

"So what's the point of this, Mark, I've already been shown how active she was before her illness?"

"No, Matthew, this is after I treated her."

"Bollocks, Mark!"

"Look, Matthew, I'm telling you it is!"

"Are you serious?" Matthew gasped.

"Yes I am"

"Well fuck me Mark!"

"I'll debate theology with you all night but I'll draw the line at that. I said I didn't want to fight you, but if I've got a choice, fight you I will, Matthew."

They both laughed but Matthew stopped, he was remembering what he had just witnessed, he was in shock.

Mark carried on with his explanation about his exile on the island. "I had a second meeting with the Federal Medical Council and I presented this video as proof of my treatment but they still wouldn't sanction it."

"I don't understand how they could deny it was a cure?"

"I thought the same but they explained it away, as being one of those weird medical freaks, that we've all heard of, you know the type of thing we read in the papers, that someone who was given a short time to live and that they couldn't be given anymore treatment and everything they had already been given had failed to cure them. Suddenly they go into remission and make a full recovery. Or the blind patient who's been blind from childhood, who suddenly regains their sight. The media call it a miracle, an act of God and that's how the medical authorities explained this away."

"You're kidding?"

"No I'm not and I was threatened that if I released this information, I would be struck off as a practising doctor and publically humiliated. I would be labelled a quack and nothing more than a charlatan. They continued to ban me from carrying on with my research anywhere in the US that's why I'm still here and why I'm being hunted down."

"The bastard's!"

Matthew said to Mark "surely you didn't just accept their decision did you?"

"I had no option other than to continue my research in exile until I was ready to challenge them and expose them for what they are; I hired a private investigator, to see if he could find out anything, which I could use against them."

"Did he?"

"Yes he found out that all of them had embezzled the health department out of money by claiming false expenses and the chairman had actually had a considerable amount of work carried out on his Beverly Hills home financed by the health authority."

"So why haven't you already exposed them to the authorities over this?"

"I needed to find someone like you to help me to expose them about my treatment first. So will you help me Matthew?"

"Without doubt of course I will."

"So how do you actually feel now, Matthew?"

"I'm really pissed off, Mark. I just don't know what to say other than I can't believe this."

"OK, so what are you going to do about it?"

"I've not got a clue at the moment but you can be sure they're going to regret ever hearing the name Matthew Michellin."

"That's the spirit, Matthew, but you'll need to be very careful of how you go about this and just what information you let people have. Whatever you do, you mustn't reveal where my clinic is or where I am otherwise they'll destroy all the evidence I have."

"OK I understand, Mark. No one will ever hear from me where you are, whatever they do to me but just in case they find you, why don't you give me a copy of everything you have evidence wise, especially the tape of Sarah."

"Good idea I'll do that but you will have to be very careful who you involve in this, you must choose wisely. I know it sounds dramatic but don't trust anyone Matthew, not even your family, you don't want to make them a target do you? Be careful of strangers you meet, the guy in the bar you strike up a conversation with or the pretty girl. However innocent they seem, they could be the enemy. Always try to be around people you know, just assume you haven't got a friend in the world other than me."

"You are really starting to put the shits up me now, Mark."

"I'm sorry, just as long as you're careful you'll be OK."

"I will, don't worry. I'm not a fool and once I've let the cat out of the bag nobody will be brave enough to come after me."

"Listen, Matthew, if think about the implications of releasing this to the general public, the governments responsible for this suppression, will be under attack by all the people affected by what they have done. I'm talking riots in the street, public outcry and protests even demands for new elections, by the thousands of people who have suffered. Just imagine for every death or still recovering victim, such as yourself, there could be at least ten family members or friends who will want answers and that could add up to tens of, if not hundreds of thousands of people and that means these bastards can't refuse what we want."

"That's right."

"Matthew, Can I ask you a question?"

"Of course you can."

"Can you tell me the name of your Russian friend?"

"I'm sorry, Mark, I can't."

"What, why can't you?"

"I just can't!"

"Why?"

"Look I just can't."

"Stop messing about, Matthew. What's she called?"

"I'm not messing about."

"So tell me her name will you?"

Matthew remained silent.

"Why won't you just tell me? You've never introduced her to me. I've never heard you mention her name. What's going on?"

"I can't remember it, that's why" Matthew yelped.

Mark was stunned and confused. "What do you mean you can't remember it?"

"You see I've got a terrible memory for names so I have to revert to word association."

"So what have you associated her name with?"

"I've forgot that as well."

"How can you forget her name?"

"It's just something that's happened since I fell ill, my memory has become terrible, especially for names and once I've slept with them there just doesn't seem to be a need to know their names any longer."

"Matthew, you're a jerk, I'll just have to find it out myself then."

Matthew didn't know what else to say other than, "Good idea, Mark, and when you do can you let me know what she's called?" Matthew smiled and shrugged his shoulders, this was a trait that some people found endearing as this cheeky idiosyncrasy normally melted the hearts of most women but usually pissed off most men, just as it had now pissed off Mark.

"You're a clown, Matthew!"

It came the time for Matthew to return to the UK. While the last couple of days of his holiday, had almost turned his life upside down, not only by what Mark had told him but he just couldn't get the video of Sarah out of his mind and he couldn't concentrate on anything, other than how he was going to expose this conspiracy to the world and during this time he completely ignored his goddess, so much so that she told him she wasn't going back to the UK with him and that she had asked Mark if he could help get her a nursing job at the islands hospital and that she intended to stay on the island, at least for the rest of the European winter. She had started to think Matthew had lost interest in her, owing to his recent behaviour towards her and when she asked him what was wrong, he was unable to tell her what was bothering him, as he had promised Mark he would only discuss this with people who could help him with this problem. They both accepted that a break would be a good thing, she would gain valuable nursing experience and he didn't need any distraction from his determination to bring about this exposé. They did agree, however that when she returned to Manchester, they would take up from where they had left off.

Her thoughts were, of how great it would be when they did get back together and what a night of passion that would be. Whereas Matthew's thoughts had already turned to what he was going to do about this enforced period of celibacy and he was thinking of how many different names he was going to forget of before she returned.

Chapter 3
Matthew and his Big Mouth

Checking in at the airport for his Virgin Atlantic Boeing 747, flight to Manchester, Matthew had the pleasant surprise to find that Mark had upgraded his ticket to first class.

It was the first time Matthew had flown first class. He was welcomed aboard the aircraft by a beautiful stewardess, who led him to the first class cabin and to his seat, or more like to his bed. The seat he had converted into a bed and it had its own entertainment system and he could even draw curtains around himself for his own privacy. For Matthew they were a waste, as he had no intention of missing anything that happened during this flight, or concealing himself from the gaze of other people, if people wanted to see him he was going to let them because some of those people may be very attractive ladies. The stunning stewardess brought him a blanket and a pillow. She asked him if he had travelled in first class before.

"Yes I have many times," he lied to her.

She replied, "If that's the case there is no need in telling you how everything works then is there, sir?"

"Well a quick reminder wouldn't go amiss."

She leaned across him. The top two buttons on her shirt were open, exposing just enough flesh and cleavage to be classy but not trampish. There was a delicious smell about her, which he recognised immediately, as Beverly Hills by Charley. Matthew used to know someone he once worked with who wore this perfume all the time and whenever he smelt it he was reminded of her, ironically he couldn't remember her name either.

The female attendant offered him a glass of champagne, which he readily accepted.

"I would prefer a Manhattan though if you don't mind."

"Let's see what we can do about that when we are in flight, have you enjoyed your trip to the island, sir?"

Matthew took this opportunity to flirt with her.

"Yes, I have thank you but it would have been much better, if I would have been there with someone as gorgeous as you."

"Thank you, sir," she replied.

She continued "and have you been to the island before?

"No I haven't, this is my fist trip but I do think I will probably be coming back in a couple of months and maybe if you're on my flight, we could have a drink in the airport lounge during your turn around?"

"I'm sorry, sir, were not allowed to drink prior to a flight."

"What about some time in Manchester then?" He wouldn't be put off as he was thinking of his period of enforced celibacy.

Well, sir, we will have to see about that later." She smiled at him and quickly tried to change the subject. "Were you on the island for business, or pleasure?"

"A little bit of both you could say."

"Was it successful trip?"

"I think so, but time may tell."

"What business are you in, sir, if you don't mind me asking?"

Smiling he replied, "I'm a drug smuggler." He looked at her straight face and seeing how shocked she was, he put her mind at ease and laughed.

"I'm only joking. I'm a journalist and an author. Anyway, if we are meeting up for a drink in Manchester, we need to know each other's name."

"I'm sorry, sir, I didn't say we were, I said I'd think about it."

"Come on you know we will be; I'm Matthew and you are?"

"Andrea." She was now smiling.

"That's a lovely name."

Discreetly, without her seeing, he wrote her name on a napkin she had given him with his champagne, ensuring he didn't forget it, at least not for now anyway.

Once they had taken off he pressed the overhead buzzer. Andrea arrived in seconds still smiling.

"You promised me a Manhattan when we were in flight, Andrea."

"OK I will get you that now, would you like ice with that, sir?"

"Yes please." She smiled at him and walked down the aisle. Matthew had a feeling that he was "cracking her."

She returned a few minutes later, cocktail in hand. Her smile was incredible and her face perfect.

When she left, Matthew picked up the drink and while sipping it, he noticed the napkin which she had placed down had her name and a phone number on it. Matthew smiled to himself, he was full of pride.

About a half hour later, Andrea was walking towards his end of the cabin. He grabbed her arm in a delicate way. She stopped and flirtatiously rolled her eyes.

"Yes, Matthew, how can I help you?"

"So I guess you are taking me up on my offer then?"

"That depends if you ring me."

"I can promise you I will; do you like Chinese food?"

"Yes it's my favourite."

"How about coming with me to China Town?"

"Yes, that sounds good."

"OK we know where, how about when?"

"Ring me next Friday and I will know my shift pattern's by then."

Following landing, Matthew walked to the exit. There was a member of ground crew waiting for him with a wheelchair, as he struggled with walking long distances. He pushed Matthew through passport control, to baggage reclaim and then to the nearest taxi rank. Once outside the Airport, Matthew frantically searched for his cigarettes and lighter, like an asthmatic would do, while they were struggling to find their nebuliser, as they were fighting for breath. By the time Matthew eventually got into a taxi, which took no more than five minutes, he had managed to smoke three cigarettes. Once inside the taxi he referred to his notes and formulated a plan about what he intended to do with this stem cell thing and to be honest he was still utterly confused about what any of this meant.

Once he arrived home, Matthew went into his office and searched details about politicians. He decided he should approach his local Member of Parliament, who was a member of the opposition and appeared to be a rather insignificant member at that, which suited Matthew. Matthew emailed him asking if they could meet, as he had some delicate information which he may be interested in. He decided to leave it at that, as he didn't want to be giving anything away at this point.

The following morning Matthew found an email, in reply to his. He had been invited to a meeting at 11 a.m. at the MP's surgery the following Saturday. Matthew thought to himself how he needed to be extremely cautious, as he recalled how Mark advised him to be careful of whom he involved in this scheme. He spent the whole of the day composing a comprehensive manuscript, in which he recorded everything Mark had told him and more. He printed two copies of the manuscript and put them in two separate manila envelopes, on which he wrote his details. Matthew sealed both of them with wax. He recalled how many years beforehand his grandfather had explained that this was a method used so the owner could always see if the seal had been broken and the contents accessed. His grandfather also explained how in the wax you would leave a personal impression, as people could always reseal the envelope trying to hide the fact it had been opened but they wouldn't be able to recreate the impression, making the contents of the envelope even safer, his grandfather used a ring which had his initials on. As Matthew didn't have a ring to make his impression with, he looked around the room for something to use as his personal impression, with nothing else to hand, he used the top off a bottle of Jack Daniels as his ID mark.

He decided that he was going to leave both copies of the manuscript with his solicitor Simon, who was also his financial advisor and someone who had been a close friend of Matthews for over 30 years and someone who he trusted with his life, which ironically Matthew was now planning to do. Matthew made an appointment to have lunch with him the following day, at a restaurant where he was well known.

When he entered the restaurant, Simon was already there. He shook Simon's hand and they sat at a table and ordered their food and a drink. Matthew ordered a jug of Manhattan, the waitress asked, "Did you say a full jug, sir?"

"Yes I did," replied Matthew.

"Do you realise how much that will cost you, sir?"

When the waitress told him how much the jug would cost, he nearly fell off his chair, it was almost ten times what he had been paying on St Kitts. *Robbing bastards* he thought.

Matthew took the two envelopes from his briefcase. He didn't tell Simon about his meeting with Mark, however he explained to him, that he had got himself into a delicate situation and was sorry he couldn't explain to him what it was. Matthew handed him the two envelopes and asked him not to open them but keep them safely locked away and that he felt his life could be in danger. He said to Simon, if he was informed that something had happened to him, however natural it may seem he should give these manuscripts to two separate national tabloids.

"Look, Matthew, I don't, know what you've managed to get yourself involved in but as your legal representative and your friend I would advise you to go to the authorities." Simon looked increasingly concerned.

"Unfortunately I can't do that, you see it's the authorities that I could be in trouble with."

"OK Matthew but you know that I can't get involved with anything criminal or against the law."

"Don't worry. I promise you it's nothing like that."

"Matthew, you know I need more than that?"

"Look don't push me, Si. I've said that I can't tell you, it's just that I've got some extremely delicate information that these people want."

"OK well if you want me to do this for you, is there anyone who may legitimately want these manuscripts in the future?"

"No not that I can think of."

"OK maybe not now but just in case there may be, I think we should think of a code word, which they would need to tell me before I released them."

"Good idea, I tell you what let's agree on "bastards" as the code word." Matthew thought this was fitting.

"So if anyone asks you for this other than me, they will have to know the code word is bastards."

Simon agreed to the code word and noted it in his diary.

"Just how long do you think you will leave this with me?"

"I couldn't say really but as we agreed before if you hear that I've died in a road traffic accident, or under any circumstances, even natural causes you must give them to the press. Or if you hear that anything has happened to Dr Mark Cooper and you can't contact me, you need to do what we've agreed and give them, not post them but give them to the press."

"OK well look after yourself, Matthew. Please be careful with whatever you have got yourself involved in."

"I'll try, thanks a lot, Si, I must get home now, as I have some people to talk to." Matthew suddenly felt a little better, not safer just better. Now the next thing was to prepare for his appointment with his MP.

The morning of Matthew's meeting arrived and he walked into his MP's office to meet a small untidy looking man, who was already sat down at his desk and talking on the phone. He didn't even look up to acknowledge Matthew, he continued talking, ignoring Matthew completely. His only attempt to make Matthew realise he was aware someone had walked into his office, was to raise his free hand and make a gesture to whoever it may be to sit down. Matthew took an instant dislike to the guy. The MP, Frank Davy, was dressed in a scruffy, creased black suit and off white shirt, his shirt was open at the collar which was frayed at the edges, he wore no tie and his jacket shoulders were covered in thousands of specks of dandruff. Matthew sat down at the other side of his untidy desk, there was a sweet sickly smell about him and he couldn't have been more repulsive if he tried. Anyhow this odious little character was Matthew's only salvation, so he decided to ignore the guy's ignorant manner and be as respectful to him as he would be to anyone. Once the guy had finished his conversation, he looked up at Matthew.

"So you want my help do you I have to advise you, I don't know anything about disabled rights or what you're entitled to. All that I can suggest is you go to the Citizen's Advice Bureau."

Matthew was furious. *What an arsehole* Matthew thought to himself, however he managed to keep his cool.

Just because I've got a walking stick and a bad limp, this bastard thinks I'm here to sponge from the state. After a second or two, Matthew began to feel proud of himself as he wouldn't normally let people get away with a comment like that. In most situations he would have given him a right mouthful, probably just stopping short of punching him in the mouth. Matthew wasn't a violent man but idiots like him would normally push him into a side of his personality, which he really didn't like about himself. He realised, though, that this piece of shit had something, that Matthew wanted, which was access to the Prime Minister.

Matthew went on to explain, "I have some delicate information I need to discus with the Prime Minister and I was hoping you could arrange a meeting between us."

Through his body language you could tell he couldn't care less. He sat there, just eyeing Matthew up with contempt. The type of contempt, Matthew assumed the guy would have saved for someone who had the nerve to ask him to take a shower.

"Oh yes and why do you think the Prime Minister would want to talk to someone like you?"

Matthew could again feel Mr Hyde beginning to morph but unlike before, this time he was unable to hold his tongue.

"What do you mean someone like me; someone disabled is that what you mean? Even before I spoke, you assumed all I was after was a hand-out. I don't want, or need your pity, your charity, or your pompous patronising attitude either."

Matthew realised that he would gain nothing by insulting this piece of shit but he could feel his body begin to tighten up and his right hand had transformed into a tight fist. It took all the willpower and determination he could muster not to stand up and deck this prick but all that would do is leave him dead in the water. He would just have to be patient and wait to thump him once all this was over. Frank was shocked by the anger in Matthew's tone.

"What I need to tell him, I am sure he would prefer to hear from me, rather than read about it in the tabloids, you see what I have to inform him of, could be a threat to national security." Matthew now had his total attention.

"I think you should let me be the judge of that, so I think you need to tell me what you have."

"How do I know, that I can trust you?"

"It was you who contacted me in the first place; also it seems to me you have no other choice if you want to meet the PM."

This smelly little shit knew he had the upper hand, so Matthew sat back and took a deep breath and decided he had no option other than to tell him.

Matthew had to rely on him to take this straight to the PM and not to mention it to anyone else. He had given Matthew his assurance that he would keep his word, so Matthew decided to give him an abridged account of his conversation with Mark. He left out all times, dates and places, however he did mention Mark by name and as soon as he had, he could have bitten his own tongue off. *Me and my big mouth,* he thought to himself.

Frank now stood up and came around to the front of the desk, where Matthew could now see just how scruffy he was. His shoes looked like they hadn't seen polish, since they were new and his heels were worn down to half of the thickness they were meant to be. No wonder his party had kept him out of the public eye. Matthew had a horrible feeling about this guy but he had no alternative other than to trust him. He asked him if he thought, he could get him a meeting with the PM.

"I'll have to talk to—"

Matthew quickly cut him off. "Hang on you said you wouldn't say anything to anyone."

"I won't, but what I was about to say, is that I will have to talk to the cabinet secretary, to see if he will ask the PM on your behalf."

Matthew didn't believe the smelly little tramp.

"So how quickly do you think you can do that, as it is important?"

"I will let you know as soon as it's arranged, leave me your mobile number and I'll ring you as soon as I know."

There was no way Matthew was giving his number to this little piece of shit.

"My mobile number, I'm sorry I don't have one. I wonder if you would e-mail me as soon as you can get a meeting arranged."

"I'll do that."

"Thanks only I'm going on holiday in four weeks so if it can be arranged before then, I would appreciate it."

"I'll let you know as soon as I have the details."

Matthew left thinking to himself *I have had made big mistake* but he put it down to paranoia. He had no other choice, what's done is done, he thought, *I will just have to wait and see now*.

Chapter 4
Don't Insult my Intelligence

Matthew's mistrust of Frank was well founded. As soon as Matthew left his office, the scheming little shit was already on his phone talking to his party leader, about what he had just been told. He was hoping it would earn him some much needed credibility with his party leader as he held a desire to become a member of the shadow cabinet. His party leader told him to immediately get a flight to London, so they could talk face to face about Matthew.

As leader of the opposition he realised he had a duty of care and he had to inform the PM of everything he had been told about Matthew.

Even though his views and politics were completely opposite to the PM's, both men had been good friends for years, since their days together as students at Oxford. Both men in their youth were powerful athletes and had rowed for the university against Cambridge on three separate occasions. Unfortunately on each occasion they lost the boat race but the opposition leader, Patrick Blackley always insisted to his friend the PM Jonathan Titmus that taking part was the main thing and that winning was secondary. Prime Minister Titmus's reply was the same every time.

"What a load of bollocks that is. Winning is everything and that's why your leader of the opposition!"

Patrick contacted Prime Minister Titmus and arranged to meet him in Downing Street. He told him all about the conversation he had, had with Frank and when he left the meeting, the Prime Minister, contacted the President of the USA President Willard Peterson. He informed him that they had been contacted by someone who has information about Dr Mark Cooper. The President almost choked on his coffee, he had been trying to track Mark down for the last two years and this is the first lead they had, had.

They spoke by conference call for the next hour. Both men agreed that whatever it took, Matthew Michellin had to be tracked down so they could locate Dr Cooper. They agreed that Matthew had to be taken into custody as soon as possible. The President asked the Prime Minister, as this concerns Dr Cooper, an American citizen, would he allow him to send two CIA agents to the UK to help locate Matthew and persuade him to divulge the information. The PM agreed, as long as they had no firearms and no violence involved. The President agreed and he later contacted David Prendergast, Director of National intelligence (**DNI**) and informed him of what had just happened and to immediately dispatch his two most trusted agents to the UK. The President however left out the no firearms and no violence agreement.

The two agents were immediately dispatched to the UK, where they met their equivalents from MI5, it was decided that both agencies would work separately to one another in order to track Matthew down, as it would be more beneficial operating as two groups, as they may have better success in locating him than they would if they were just one combined group. It was agreed that all of Matthew's cell calls should be monitored and any information gathered should be shared between the two agencies. They knew where he lived and that he was in this part of the UK but rather than abduct him from his home which could attract too much attention from his neighbours, they would pick him up somewhere more discreet. It was now just a waiting game. They knew it wouldn't be too long before the wait was over and it wasn't.

The following day, Matthew received a call from an old friend inviting him to meet up for a drink in one of the bars they used to frequent in Manchester city centre. Matthew phoned his brother Jim, to ask him for a lift into Manchester. Jim went berserk at him but agreed he would pick him up in 30 minutes. Matthew and his friend agreed to meet in **Yates wine lodge**[1], a down market, drinker's bar type of place, also known as **the Blob shop**. The call was intercepted and as the CIA agents were already in Manchester and the closest to Matthew, it was agreed they would pick him up.

Jim picked Matthew up from his house and when he got into the car.

Jim said "Matt, where the fuck have you been? We've all been frantic with worry."

"Look, our kid I told you I was going away for a few weeks."

"I know you did but you didn't say where too and this is the first time anyone's heard from you since you returned. We've not been able to get hold of you, what the fuck have you been up to Matt? We didn't know if you were dead or alive."

"Obviously you can see I'm alive."

"I can now you asshole, so what's going on Matt?"

"Right, well you know that Russian bird I told you about?"

"Yes I do" Jim sighed,

"Well I've been banging her in ST Kitts."

---

[1] Yates wine lodge, was always known as and still is known today, as The Blob Shop.

"Is that a euphemism our kid?"

"No you prat, the Island St Kitts!"

"So couldn't you have phoned?"

"I'm sorry I couldn't as we weren't on the same frequency as you are over here."

"What about the land line?"

"Sorry our kid I just didn't think."

"So who you meeting today, is it yet another of your conquests?"

"No it's not, do you remember Colin the electrician I used to work with years ago?"

"Yes I do."

"I'm meeting him."

"Meeting him where?"

"I'm meeting him in **The Blob Shop**, on Oldham Street."

They arrived and Matthew entered, Jim agreed to pick him up later. Matthew noticed Colin was sat at the bar. He joined him and started with a pint of Lager and a blob chaser and while they were both reminiscing about the old days, neither of them noticed the two CIA agents enter the bar but even if they had, they wouldn't have had a clue who they were anyway but they did however stand out from the normal clientele as they both wore expensive Italian tailored suits. The agents sat at a table near the door and waited for an opportunity to approach Matthew, even though they hadn't met Matthew before, they recognised who he was owing to the description they had been given of him.

Matthew stood up and made his way to the toilet, the agents followed him. Matthew stood at the urinal.

Both agents entered behind him.

One of the agents stood by his side and said "Hello Matthew."

Matthew turned to look at who was there.

"Sorry do I know you?"

"No you don't but you and I do have a mutual friend so to speak."

"Who's that?"

"A certain Dr Mark Cooper that's who."

Matthew nearly pissed all over his trousers but tried to act un-nerved.

"Who did you say?"

"I said Dr Mark Cooper."

"I don't know him."

"Look, Matthew, we know that you have just spent some time with him and we want to know where he is."

"I've got no idea who or where he is."

"Matthew we're not here to mess about, we're here to get some information from you and you would be well advised to co-operate if you know what's good for you."

"Hang on what do you mean if I know what's good for me?"

"Matthew, we know you're not a fool, so don't act like one."

"I'm not acting like a fool, I don't know what you're talking about."

"Look we don't care how you want to play this, that's your choice but if I was you I would make it easy on yourself and admit you do and tell us where he is."

"I don't understand what you want with me, you must be confusing me with someone else, I've never heard of the bloke."

"Look stop being a fucking asshole and do yourself a favour."

"Bollocks pal I don't know who you are, so just leave me alone will you." Matthew protested, "All I did was come in here for a piss and I've got you asking me about some bloke I've never heard of."

The agent who had been doing all the talking reached into his pocket and took a revolver from it and held it to Matthews head.

Matthew suddenly went cold with fear. He had no idea who these guys were but he knew he was in deep shit whoever they were.

"Look I'm telling you the truth. I have never heard of this doctor bloke, so leave me alone will you."

Matthew was aware of a second man dressed similar to the man who was holding the gun to his head.

The second guy said, "Look you will tell us eventually, so why not save yourself a lot of grief and just tell us where he is?"

As scared as he was, his brain began to clear and take control. He had imagined this scenario lots of times in his head since he had left the island and just how he would handle it when it happened. He had promised Mark he would never divulge anything about him, so he needed to be brave and keep his word.

"I've told you already, I don't have a clue a who you're talking about."

"OK, Matthew, we'll do this the hard way if that's what you want."

The agent with the gun hit Matthew hard in the stomach, he then grabbed him by the back of his hair and pulled him away from the urinal, he punched Matthew in the face. Matthew tried to defend himself but it was futile, as he only had the one good arm and that was for holding his walking stick. He tried anyway and in doing so lost his balance and fell onto the floor. While he lay there he used his walking stick and hit the other agent, the one without the gun, cross the shin bone of his left leg, the agent let out an agonising scream which could be heard in the bar. Colin ran into the toilet but once he had seen what was happening he turned and ran out again.

Matthew thought *I see that you're still the shithouse you always was then Col*, the agent with the gun followed Colin back into the bar.

"If you know what's good for you, just forget what you've seen in there and go somewhere else right now."

"What about Matthew?"

"I've just told you, forget about what you've seen, we're old friends of Matthew, so we will take care of him. So go right now or stay and have some yourself got it?"

"Right, I've got it."

"Look, Matthew's told us who you are and where you live, so if you talk about this to anyone, we will make a point of calling on you one night and we won't be as gentle as we have been with Matthew."

At this point, Colin was terrified and decided the best thing would be to leave right away. He picked up his pint and spilt most of it all over himself, missing his mouth and soaking his shirt, with lager dripping from his chin; he stood and briskly made his way out of the bar and into the cold damp Manchester afternoon.

Once outside he ran as fast as his legs could carry him, to the nearest taxi rank where he climbed into a black cab and instructed the driver to take him home to Didsbury in south Manchester. He had no consideration for Matthew at all and this wasn't the first time he had done this to Matthew. He recalled one night almost thirty years before, when he and a group of friends including Matthew were having a drink in a night club in the city centre, which was full of ne'er-do-wells[2], when an argument broke out between a group and his friends about a girl. Colin decided to go to the restroom and when he exited the rest room, the club was in uproar, reminiscent of a western saloon brawl. Not wanting to get hurt, Colin ran out of the place and jumped into a **Joe**[3] and left his friends to their own devices. It was only after the weekend when he arrived at work, that he became aware of the full extent of the evening, Matthew had received two stab wounds, one to his shoulder and one in the back, which meant he had to spend the weekend in hospital. Colin remembered all his friends, including Matthew had forgiven him but he wondered whether Matthew would forgive him this time.

Meanwhile in the toilet the agents were still with Matthew.

"We need somewhere to talk to you where we won't be disturbed. So were giving you a lift home," said the agent who Matthew had almost crippled.

"Like fuck you are." Matthew was still slumped on the restroom floor.

"Look we've told you, you can make this thing easy on yourself by just cooperating with us. We can't talk to you in here can we? The best place for you to be is at home, we know your brother is picking you up later, so just phone him and tell him he needn't bother."

"Bollocks, I'm letting him take me home."

---

[2] A Ne'er do well is an old fashioned phrase used to describe a Rouge, vagrant or Vagabond without means of support, a good for nothing and was the subject of an 1887 play The Ne'er-do-Weel by W S Gilbert(of Gilbert and Sullivan fame) and was later renamed the Vagabond.

[3] A Joe is a nickname you hear in Manchester for a taxi, it was allegedly first coined in the 19th century and named after a frequent handsome cab user called Joe Baxi.

The agent said "Matthew you wouldn't want him to meet us, would you?"

Matthew remembered what Mark had told him about his family being a target.

"Look you bastard, whoever you are; leave my brother out of whatever this is."

"OK we will, so just tell him not to pick you up and come with us."

Matthew realised he had no alternative other than to do what he had been told, he thought *I can't even get the police involved, as I'm just jumping out of the frying pan into the fire if I do, as they would probably just hand me over to MI5, or the CIA*

"OK I'll do it."

One of the agents picked Matthew up off the floor and the three of them walked out of the toilet together, this time one agent was limping more than Matthew.

"Right let's go outside." The agent with the gun had hold of Matthew. As they got outside he pushed Matthew up against the external wall. The limping agent stayed with Matthew outside the rear entrance on Tib Street, while the agent with the gun went to get the car. Tib Street is a street in Manchester that used to be full of pet shops many, many years ago, most of which had now closed down but one or two still remained. The agent pulled up in the car. Matthew had christened him "The Nutter." They shoved Matthew into the passenger seat next to the driver. The good guy the one with the limp sat directly behind Matthew and held a commando knife to the back of his head.

"Don't try anything stupid, understand Matthew."

"OK" Matthew nodded he was becoming increasingly more nervous and he didn't have a clue how he was going to get out of this.

The 'Nutter' exited the car and walked a few yards to one of the remaining pet shops, which had little puppies in the window. He went inside and picked one and returned to the car with the pup. He climbed into the driver's seat, the "Good Guy" was wondering what was going on.

"What the fuck, are you doing?" he said.

"I've just bought our new friend Matthew a present." He continued, "I'm betting you're a dog lover aren't you Matthew?"

"Yes I am."

"See we're good guys. I've bought you a present."

He handed Matthew the dog, which immediately snuggled up on his knee. It was yapping and it crawled up his coat and started to lick his face, they both took to each other immediately. The little pup was nipping Matthew's ear, with tiny needle sharp teeth. *Better than the knife that was there a few minutes ago,* Matthew thought.

They headed towards Matthew's home, but on the way stopped at an industrial unit on a small trading estate. They all exited the car. The 'Nutter' carried the pup and they all went into the building. It was a storage depot and they went into a small front office, which was sparsely furnished with a few chairs and an empty desk. The little dog was now running around playing with pieces of paper. Matthew couldn't help but think this was the most surreal moment of his life. The agents started to quiz Matthew once again on the whereabouts of Dr Mark.

"Just how many more times do I have to tell you? I don't know him."

"Look don't insult my intelligence, you limey bastard!" "Don't try to make a fool out of me." The 'Nutter' was becoming even angrier. Matthew had been tied to a chair so he couldn't escape. The good guy decided to leave the office and take a look around the depot.

"So, you want to play tough do you?" without any warning, the 'Nutter' pistol whipped Matthew on the forehead splitting it wide open, opening up at least a six inch wound. Matthew momentarily passed out; he came round with excruciating pain in his head and blood streaming down his face. He was delirious and everything was a blur, not only due to regaining his consciousness but also because of the blood running into his eyes. While he was no hero, he still had the determination not to break his promise to Mark. The puppy was now looking for attention and began running around Matthew and the 'Nutter', yapping wanting to play. Without warning, the 'Nutter' kicked the puppy like a football, launching it through the air and hitting the far wall, the puppy was now yelping in obvious pain.

"You rotten bastard," Matthew gasped. He realised that whoever these two were, they weren't the type of government official, if that's who they were, that you thought would protect you if you were in trouble, you wouldn't want these two too arrive at your door if you called 911 or 999, you would have preferred the "Stasi," the East German secret police, or even the "Gestapo" to be the ones who arrived, rather than these two psychopaths, *who the fuck were they* he thought. The 'Nutter' then punched Matthew on the jaw, so hard he felt two teeth coming loose inside his mouth. He was now not only bleeding badly from his head wound but now also from his mouth. Matthew said, "Look you can do whatever you want but I can't tell you something I don't know, you can even kill me if you like."

"Matthew we're not here to kill you, if we were your family would already be placing flowers on your grave."

The 'Nutter' said "Have you ever seen the film *Reservoir Dogs*, Matthew?"

"Yes I have."

"Do you remember the scene with the cop in the warehouse?"

He took his commando knife from his belt and held it at the side of Matthew's head.

"You wouldn't do that, you bastard."

"Try me if you want."

He punched Matthew again, this time splitting his flesh just below the eye.

"Make sure that's the last time you call me a bastard. Look this is just the start of things to come."

Matthew was scared shitless but he remembered once reading that in a situation like this, the last thing to do was to show you were scared and you should be as aggressive as you're captor, as it confuses them and they won't know how to handle it. So he said, "Why are you a bastard by birth or what?" The guy went berserk and kept hitting Matthew around the head. Matthew thought *what a load of shite that book was.*

"Matthew we're he to make sure you come to no harm and to protect you."

Matthew said, "are you taking the piss or what, see I come to no harm, I feel like I've just gone twelve rounds, with Mike fucking Tyson."

"Look, Matthew we're the good guys, if it wasn't us it would be someone else who wouldn't be as gentle as we have been with you."

Matthew said, "Get fucked you're just a pair of fucking psychopaths."

The good guy re-entered the office and saw Matthew was bleeding badly.

He said, "Leave him for now give him a break, we need to get that wound on his head looked at, he needs to go to hospital and have it treated."

The 'Nutter' said "we can't take him to hospital; we will have to do it ourselves."

"How can we do that?"

The 'Nutter' replied, "when I was in special, forces I was trained to treat wounds like that on wounded colleagues and even on myself. So it's not a problem for me at least."

"So do we have the stuff to do it?"

"Yes it's in the car."

"Let's get it then."

The 'Nutter' said "hang on before we go give me a minute with him by myself." He asked Matthew "how do you like your present?" The good guy went out of the office again.

"She's a lovely little thing." Matthew replied.

Matthew whistled and the pup started to move towards him from where it had landed, it was limping and whimpering and in terrible pain, it looked a sorry sight as it made its way over to him. The 'Nutter' picked the dog up violently, he held it by the scuff of the neck and took his commando knife from his belt and held it to the pup's throat and gestured as if he was going to kill it; the pup was still whimpering in pain, he said to Matthew.

"So how much do you like this dog?" and he again made as if he was going to kill it.

"You wouldn't do that, you bastard!"

"I told you about calling me that, now tell us what we want to know."

Matthew shouted "Fuck off you psychotic bastard," not considering this would push him over the edge, what happened next shocked Matthew, even after all he had been through he couldn't believe that this 'Nutter' was capable of doing what he did next. Matthew cringed in horror as he watched the 'Nutter' slit the dog's throat and throw it against the wall.

"Wouldn't I?" he said while laughing out loud and his eye's looked Demonic, full of hatred and evil. Matthew realised his latest insult had gone too far, he felt sick as he watched the pup's nervous system still working as it lay there dying on the floor it was still twitching and It's back legs were kicking out. The second agent came back in and said. "There was no need for that, come and help me bring in the stuff from the car," they both went out of the room for a couple of minutes leaving Matthew sat where he was, as much as he tried he couldn't remove his gaze from the poor pup. After a short time they both returned. Both were carrying bags, the good one also had what appeared to be a bowl of hot water, they both placed the things they were carrying on the desk, the good guy started to bathe and clean the cut to Matthews forehead, he then started to cut the hair around the wound, with scissors he had taken from the bag, he produced a cut throat razor.

Matthew thought, oh for fuck's sake, what now. Matthew started to tremble and wondered just how much more he could take without blowing Mark's cover. This was one of the times when his hypocritical side kicked in as he started to pray as hard as he could, he was that scared he would have even made a pact with the devil at this moment for nothing to happen, however the agent only shaved around the cut, he then took a bottle of brandy from the bag, opened it and poured it onto the wound, Mathew felt a small tingle.

Matthew said, "That was a waste, I would have preferred to drink that."

The agent untied Matthew's right arm and gave him the bottle, Matthew took a large gulp of the brandy, it was cheap shit, not what he had become accustomed to while on St Kitts, he then caught sight of what the 'Nutter' was doing, he was threading a needle, Mathew *thought oh shit* and grabbed the brandy and took another long drink, the good agent was making sure Mathew was tied tight enough, but left his right arm free and he placed a piece of cloth between Matthews teeth and covered his mouth with gaffer tape, so any screams he made could not be heard outside the unit.

The very next moment the 'Nutter' was standing in front of him with his needle and thread. Matthew thought *oh shit this is going to hurt,* the good guy was standing at the back of Matthew holding him down. Matthew thought *can't you just knock me out somehow*, then the excruciating pain began, as he first felt the needle being forced through his skin on one side of the wound, then through the other side, if that wasn't bad enough when he started to pull the thread through the holes in Matthew's skin not only did it hurt, it made him feel like he was going to throw up, he felt him tie a knot, then the good guy poured more brandy into the cut, he handed the bottle to Matthew and took the tape off Matthews mouth who took another long drink of brandy,

The 'Nutter' was putting another stitch into Matthew's head but for some reason this one felt a lot less painful than the first one, maybe because he was getting pissed, then thank God it was over, the good guy said "that's it your done now, so let's get back to talking about Dr Cooper shall we?"

Matthew took a very long drink of the brandy, almost a quarter of the bottle in one gulp, all it did was make him cough and want to throw up again.

The 'Nutter' left the office and went to the toilet the good agent said "Come on Matthew let's stop messing around and just tell us what we want to know for your own sake, you've seen what my friend is capable of, just don't make him angry as I don't know what he could do if he gets angry but I can tell you it won't be pleasant."

"Fuck you both, you're nothing more than a pair of psychopathic bastards."

"Now, now, Matthew, don't be like that we're just trying to help you, you know."

"So why don't you just kill me if you're going to?"

"Matthew were not going to kill you, were here to, protect you. There are a lot nastier people out there who will be looking for you, so why not trust us and do yourself a favour."

"I heard you say before you were Special Forces, what would Special Forces be doing coming after me?"

"No Matthew, were not Special Forces we're CIA."

"Hang on I didn't think the CIA tortured people."

"We don't torture people."

"So what the fuck do you call what you've been doing to me?"

"Were, just trying to protect you, Matthew and see you come to no harm"

"What with two broken teeth, an embroidered skull, almost blind in one eye and a poor dead puppy in the corner some fucking minders you two are."

"I tell you what, Matthew, if it had been someone other than us you would know what torture is really like. You're lucky we've kept you from experiencing that."

"I'm sorry about my manners," said Matthew, "I can't thank you enough, for what you've done to help keep me from being hurt."

The 'Nutter' came back into the room, mocking Matthew by making a sound of a dog barking and he was laughing.

The good agent decided he would now go to the toilet and limped out of the office, still feeling some discomfort from being hit by Matthew in the toilet back at Yates's, Matthew was once again alone with the "Nutter."

The 'Nutter' said "Do you like to gamble, Matthew?"

"No not really."

"That's a shame, as I thought we would play a little game of roulette, the Russian kind," the "Nutter laughed and took the revolver from his pocket and fitted it with a silencer and placed one bullet in the chamber and spun the chamber around, he walked over to Matthew, he placed the gun to his genitals and pulled the trigger, no loud noise no pain.

Matthew breathed a sigh of relief and said "you're a fucking idiot."

The 'Nutter' started to laugh even more.

"Well that was lucky but the odds, are now getting shorter." He placed the gun there again.

For some reason probably to show he wasn't fazed by what was happening. Matthew started to whistle Colonel Bogey[4].

The good guy re- entered the office and said.

"Stop messing about with him put the gun down will you; we've got to leave now."

Matthew said "so what then more torture or what?"

"No I think you've had enough of that for now."

"What next then?"

"Were, taking you on a nice little trip."

---

[4] Colonel Bogey is the tune whistled in the film The Bridge over the river Kwai and the British soldier's sang the words to the tune (Hitler has only got one ball).

"Can I ask where to?"

"Yes of course you can, were taking you to that meeting you've been so keen to have, were taking you to Ten Downing Street and you're going to meet your Prime Minister and to have a chat with our President."

The 'Nutter' started to pack everything away and he put the dead pup into a carrier bag and took everything to the car, throwing the pup into a skip which was outside the depot.

"So how do we get there?"

The agent said "were flying there." He then said "Mathew I've heard you're a bit of a ladies man?"

"I wouldn't say that."

"What would you say then?"

"I'm just a sociable type of guy that's all."

"Matthew, I think that where you'll eventually end up going, you're likely to be doing a fair bit of socialising."

"I can't go like this."

"I know, were now going to take you home, so you can freshen up and I would bring enough clothes for about a week, if you need them for any longer you can always get them dry cleaned or buy some more but once you've freshened up, I think you'll need to put your best clothes on and bring with you or wear a tie."

He continued by saying, "Look, Matthew, seeing as now we really are friends here's a phone number for you."

"Hang on this is a Washington phone number, what would I want with this?"

"Matthew, I'm betting you'll end up there sooner rather than later and just in case you find yourself alone one night and in need of some company, you won't find any better hookers anywhere in the states than there."

"Well thanks."

"There you are, Matthew, I told you we we're your friends, just a heads up, they're all drop dead gorgeous but there's one in particular called Georgia, she's quite a bit older than the other girl's but you know what they say about an old fiddle don't you?"

"Yes I do, but is she clean."

"Of course she is; she gets retuned every week. She maybe a bit longer in the tooth than you would normally expect but I recommend her and all the others are also medically checked every 7 days and if you do end up in Washington, you'll probably stay at the Willard hotel, there's three of the waitresses, who work there, tell them I've sent you and you'll be really looked after if you know what I mean?"

"I hope I do but the problem is I don't know your name."

"I'm Giovanni, an Italian immigrant's son."

"What about the psychopath?"

"Oh he's just referred to as the Dolf he's of German extraction."

"Well the real Dolf could have learnt something about brutality from him. He's a fucking psychopath."

"I'd just be careful around him if I was you, as he hate's being called a bastard or psycho, so just be careful as I won't always be around to keep him as nice as he's been today and believe me you wouldn't want to be anywhere near him, when he turns nasty."

"Thanks for that."

"You're welcome, Matthew, look we need to get going now if we're to get to Number 10 on time. We need to get to the Airport as soon as we can."

On arrival at the airport they sat at the bar in the departures area, the three of them were going through the food Menu. Matthew was drinking Manhattan's, he ordered a fillet steak Rossini with a side of pasta, while it was being cooked a waitress set a table for them in the restaurant, she placed a jug of Manhattans on it, in the meantime Matthew announced he needed to use the restroom. He said, "I'm going by myself."

Dolf said, "Don't try anything stupid."

Matthew entered the rest room and stood at the urinals, suddenly two strangers entered the restroom they stood either side of Matthew, one of them grabbed him by the hair and smashed his head against the wall and there was a sickening thud. Matthew fell to the floor, the guy who had assaulted Matthew started to kick him around the head, the other guy knelt down by his side and started to punch Matthew in the face and said to him, "You're a dead man if you don't tell us where Dr Cooper is," the blows were sickeningly loud and painful.

He lay there *wondering where the hell, was Batman and Robin when he needed them.*

At the bar Giovanni said, "He's been a long time. I'm going to see where he is."

Both of them walked towards the restroom, Dolf said "I've got a gut feeling something isn't right, so let's get in there quickly."

They both burst through the door, just like the cape crusader and his ward, they both burst into action. Dolf jumped over Matthew and grabbed the guy who was still punching him and snapped the guy's neck like a dried twig, killing him instantly. Giovanni grabbed the other guy and pinned him down on the floor at the side of Matthew, Dolf also grabbed the guy and he then took his commando knife from his belt and in his trademark way slit the guy's throat. Both assailants were now dead. Dolf gabbed the dead guy with the broken neck and dragged him into a cubicle and he then grabbed the other guy and dragged him into a different cubicle, he came out with the IDs, of both men and announced.

"The Mossad, Israeli bastards."

Giovanni said, "I told you, Matthew, there would be others." They helped him stand up, he decided to freshen up before going back into the restaurant. At the sink while washing his face he felt something in his mouth, he spat out two teeth, four teeth lost in one day. He checked in the mirror that none of his front teeth had been knocked out, even in these circumstances he was more concerned about how his appearance was and that his smile hadn't been affected, rather than the situation he was in. Giovanni left the restroom and went into the restaurant where he found an old table cloth, which he took back to Matthew for him to dry himself. Once he had freshened up Matthew soaked the cloth in warm water and wrapped it around the wound on his head.

They left the restroom and re-entered the restaurant and sat down at the table. It was Matthew who spoke first and said, "What the fuck was that all about?"

"Look, Matthew, you're lucky to still be alive and there will be others as well, so just finish your food and your drink," said Giovanni.

"What about the two dead guys in the restroom and you're both just sat there as if nothing has happened. Just who the fuck, are you people?"

All they said was, "CIA but you already know that." Neither of them told him what they were before they became CIA agents.

Dolf had served in the most ruthless and feared part of US Special Forces, Navy Seal's group six. This group of Commandos was the closest any country had to the UK's

SAS but was still only a poor imitation, of, the who dares wins boys, first created by Colonel David Stirling during world war11. Gio was just on the verge of completing his first year as a seal but everyone knew he didn't have it in him to be recruited into group six."

"Look, don't think about them."

"That's OK for you to say but what when somebody finds them?"

"We will be miles away by then, so just drink up, Matthew, we need to go right now."."

They left the restaurant and entered the executive VIP lounge, where they were checked in by military personnel, even though they were carrying weapons, they were allowed through, as the guards had already been told to ignore anything they were carrying. When they entered the lounge, they met the pilot of the aircraft, Captain Wilson, he was already sat at a table drinking fruit juice and he was smoking a cigarette.

Matthew was introduced to him and immediately the barman brought over a jug of Manhattan. Matthew sat down next to Captain Wilson and said, "You're smoking."

He answered, "Yes that's right."

"What about the smoking ban?"

The Captain replied, "There's no restriction in here, as this is where royalty, world leaders and VIPs come through when their flying out of Manchester."

"So you mean the bastards who make the rules don't stick to them."

"Yes that's right they don't and we will need to be going soon Matthew."

"Just let me just have a couple more cigarettes before we get on the plane."

"Don't worry, Matthew, you can smoke on there as well."

"What! How have you managed that with all the other passengers?"

"Matthew there, are no other passengers, you're on a private executive jet. Just our lovely stewardesses who will pander to your every whim."

"Lovely stewardesses you say." As soon as Matthew heard lovely stewardesses he said, "So shall we get going then?"

"Do you need assistance getting on the aircraft?" The captain asked him.

"No I should be OK thanks."

"Well I will get one of the fight crew to meet you anyway just in case."

"Thank you."

Matthew and the two agents made their way to the plane, where they were met by a beautiful brunette stewardess, who assisted Matthew onto the plane. Matthew couldn't believe his eyes, he was taken to his seat, which was larger and more comfortable than the chairs in his lounge at home, directly in front of him was an oak table, not a drop down plastic table in the seat in front which he was normally used to, also attached to the seat was a TV which turned into a video conference system. The stewardess brought him a jug of Manhattan and sat down next to him with a fruit juice, she offered him a cigarette, he enquired about her name she was called Karen.

He wanted to know everything about her, she was 17 years younger than Matthew and she wore that perfume that always reminded him of that old friend he once worked with, he was intoxicated by her, as brunettes with lovely brown eyes were always his favourite, but he still wouldn't turn his nose up at most blondes or red heads, he had even had a fling with a baldy in the past, so in essence it was women in general that was his favourite.

The plane took off, not only was he flying in luxury, he was about to meet two of the most powerful men in the world. If only his wife could see him now! If only. He felt a bit emotional all of a sudden.

A TV screen in front of him came to life and a face he didn't recognise said, "Hello Matthew," the guy had an American accent. "My name is David Prendergast, I'm the Director of National intelligence and welcome aboard your flight to meet your Prime minister, I'm looking forward to our meeting tomorrow," he said "and I hope my two colleagues have taken good care of you?"

"They work for you, do they?"

"Yes they do."

"So can you see me?"

"Yes of course I can."

Matthew removed the cloth from his head, "And can you see this on my head?"

"Yes I can."

"Well just look at the stitches done by one of your men, with just a needle and cotton and no aesthetic and not just that, I'm lucky I've still got my bollocks. He's a psychopath that Dolf."

"I'm sorry, Matthew, sometimes my men can get a bit over exuberant, I've had a word and told him to be less physical with you from now on but did they not also just save your life?"

"I suppose so."

"So there you are, Swings and roundabouts as they say in your country, don't they?"

They landed at London city airport, Matthew was fuming, that he had missed an opportunity to get Linda to meet him for a drink but what was annoying him more, was that he could still remember her name, he had the feeling when he first met her that there was a connection between them and he had hoped that because of this, he may just become the latest member of the mile high club.

Chapter 5
Downing Street

Once they exited the aircraft, they were taken by limousine direct to Number 10. Matthew didn't see the PM that evening as he was taken straight upstairs past all the portraits of previous Prime Ministers and shown to the room he was to sleep in, he was informed he would be meeting the PM at 2 p.m. the following afternoon and just like everything else he'd experienced today, the room wanted for nothing. There was even a fully equipped bar, with a readymade jug of Manhattan and a box of cigars, which he left for now, thinking he will have one sometime later and in his romantic over active mind he wondered if these could be the famous cigars once smoked by Winston Churchill? Possibly not but he told himself they were just for the hell of it and he would always tell people in the future that they were, *well what are anecdotes if not emblazoned with a bit of poetic licence other than boring*? He thought but he decided just in case he forgot later, that he would take a hand full now. He put them safely in side his jacket pocket and helped himself to a drink and got ready for bed. Before he climbed into bed, he opened up the laptop he had collected when he went to his house to freshen up and recorded all that had happened during the last 48 hours or at least everything he could remember and he emailed his notes to Mark. He poured himself another drink and tried to imagine what was going to happen at his meeting tomorrow. He lay on the bed, lit a cigarette and fell blissfully asleep.

He woke up with a start, as the cigarette burnt down between his fingers, for a minute he thought the torture had begun all over again. He fell back to sleep in a moment, the next thing there was a knock on his door.

"Would you like a full English breakfast, Mr Michellin?" a voice asked.

"Yes please and some fresh orange juice and coffee as well."

"Breakfast will be served in the breakfast room down the stairs at the end of the lobby," the voice stated.

Matthew was up, showered, shaved and dressed within 35 minutes. He was starving and the thought of a coffee and a full English breakfast was irresistible. Down the stairs he went and into a luxurious breakfast room. Everything was silver service and laid out on a long mahogany sideboard. There was everything imaginable including devilled kidneys, which he had only had the pleasure of tasting once before, while he was staying at a premier golf club located near to Macclesfield in Cheshire, many years beforehand following a corporate golf day. It was the first time that at one of this particular company's, golf days, that a regular group of attendees, a group of Scotsmen were not the last to go to bed. Matthew had been challenged that he couldn't both outstay and outdrink them; it was a challenge they were going to regret. Following a cup of coffee and a glass of orange juice, Matthew filled himself with everything that was on offer in the breakfast room, it was all delicious. He even thought of asking for a doggy bag and taking it up to his room to eat for supper that evening. He asked the waitress who came to collect his plate and serve him some more coffee, if it would be alright to do so.

"There's no need, sir, we will prepare you anything you require all evening, all you need to do is ask." she replied.

He was anxiously awaiting 2 p.m. for the meeting to start, when suddenly a guy in a grey suit entered the room.

"Good morning, Mr Michellin. The Prime Minister has asked if you wouldn't mind the meeting starting a little earlier at noon?"

"What time is it now?"

"It's 11.30 a.m. now, sir."

"That's fine by me. I just need my lap top."

"Is it in your room, sir?"

"Yes it is."

"I will bring it down for you and if you wait here for me, I will escort you to the PM's office when I return." The guy disappeared and went to fetch the lap top, a few minutes later he returned.

"Mr Michellin, would you follow me please, I have your lap top," they both left the breakfast room and walked the short distance to the PM's office, they knocked on the office door and was summoned into the room, they both went in, the PM was sat behind a large mahogany desk. Prime Minister Titmus wasn't the most charismatic of people, in fact he was the type of person who illuminated a room when he left it, the office was as you would expect it to be, the very best of everything, there was a seating area on the opposite side of the office, where five more people were sat on green leather chesterfield furniture. The PM said. "Welcome, Mr Michellin, I've been looking forward to meeting you, may I introduce you, from left to right we have David Jackson, the foreign secretary and next to him is Alexander Franklin, the home secretary, then Wilfred Morgan, secretary General MI5 Janette Kelly, Health and social Security secretary and Peter Pattern Press officer."

"Good morning to you all," said Matthew, then there was a knock on the door and short fat guy walked in. The PM said, "Mr Michellin let me introduce you to the Deputy Prime minister Malcolm Collins."

"Good day, Mr Michellin. Do you mind if we all call you Matthew?"

"No not at all."

The PM said "Matthew we believe you think you have some very important information which you think could be a threat to national security?"

"That's right I do Prime Minister."

"Matthew, would you like to tell us what would that information could be?"

"Look, Prime minister, I'm not here to play games, you know very well what information I have. If you didn't why would I have just been tortured for the last twenty four hours by two CIA agents and almost murdered by two Israeli agents and why would I find myself talking to you in Downing Street this morning?"

"That's correct, Matthew, I do have an idea what you have but we would like to hear it from you."

"If you take a good look at me Prime minister, you can see that I have a disability and that there is no reason why I shouldn't be like any other able bodied person. Other than, for the likes of people like you."

"I don't understand what you mean by that statement, Mr Michellin."

"OK if that's the way you want to play it, I may as well leave right now, you know very well what I have Prime Minister. Why have you not allowed Dr Cooper's treatment to be used to cure people for the last ten years?"

"What treatment is that then, Matthew?"

"Look, stop pissing me about, the stem cell treatment Dr Cooper has discovered, that all medical establishments have refused to sanction, just because of money and in spite of the hundreds of lives it could have saved. That's the important information you know I have, so what are you prepared to do about it, Prime minister?"

"Matthew, I will need to discuss this with someone."

"What you mean you need to get permission from your puppet master across the Atlantic?"

"Can we pause there for a moment, Matthew, while we call Washington and allow my so called puppet master to hear this? Matthew if you don't mind me, saying. You do look a bit of a mess this morning and to be in some pain, could I get you a Doctor?"

"Yes you can please."

When the Doctor arrived he examined Matthew's head first and said "My God man what's happened to your head?"

Matthew explained and the Doctor couldn't believe what Matthew told him, the Doctor gave him an injection of strong pain killers and said to the PM, "As soon as this meeting is over, I want him taken to the nearest emergency room and get him looked at."

The PM asked, "Will he be alright in the mean time?"

"He will but if this gets infected he will be in agony and of no use to anyone."

Matthew continued to tell the Doctor everything that had happened, including what they did to the puppy and the killing of the two Mossad agents.

The PM said to the head of MI5. "I would hope your men wouldn't have used those tactics, Wilfred?"

"Most, definitely not, prime minister."

Malcolm Collin's interrupted and said, "Bloody Yanks, ham fisted bastards, they're responsible for the deaths of more British troops in the Middle East than the sodding Taliban."

The PM said, "What's that got to do with it Malcolm?"

"Nothing I just wanted to make a point about the amateur bastards that's all."

"Now, now Malcolm, I don't want to hear anything like that from you or anyone else today, just remember we will be joined by them soon."

The TV monitor crackled into view and the face of President Peterson came into focus. "Good morning gentlemen," said the President. "Can I assume that we have Mr Michelin with us Prime minister?"

"Yes Mr President we have, let me introduce you. Matthew, meet the president of the USA President Willard Peterson."

"Good morning Mr President."

"Good morning Matthew, it's a pleasure to finally talk to you, can we get straight to the point of this meeting?"

"That's fine by me, sir, that's what I've been trying to do all morning."

"OK Matthew what is it you would like to achieve from this meeting?"

"For a start, that I won't be beaten up and tortured by your goons again."

"Matthew I had no idea that would happen and I even issued instructions that no harm should come to you and our two over enthusiastic agents will be fully reprimanded when they return to Washington. They did however save your life as well I am informed didn't they?"

"Yes they did, but did you hear about what they did to the puppy, OK it was only a dog but in this country Sir we don't take kindly to animal cruelty."

"Matthew I don't know what you're talking about at the moment but I assure you I will find out and take the appropriate action as soon as I have."

"OK Matthew can I ask you what you expect to achieve by demanding this meeting?"

"Sir you know what I'm doing here and what I want and that's for Dr Cooper's treatment to be accepted and used to save people's lives and improve their mobility"

"That's right I do but It's not going to be that easy Matthew, we have to consider the consequence's and how people and society will be affected by it, we can't just make a big announcement like that."

"Mr President I hoped I wouldn't have to make threats, but you've got four weeks to do something about making the treatment available, or I will make people aware of what's gone on and who is responsible, then let's see how your election campaign goes. So do you agree Mr President?"

"Yes I do, but we do want to know where Dr Cooper is."

"Why's that? So you can send people to destroy all his records and beat him up, so he won't be able to inform people of the amount of deaths you're responsible for? Well Sir you need to understand that would be pointless, as I have copies of everything hidden away and with an instruction that in the event of my death, or should anything happen to Mark, this information should be passed to the media. Then let's see how you get out of that one if you can?"

"Matthew I'm not responsible for these so called deaths, as you claim I am. You see I knew nothing of Dr

Cooper until recently and as soon as I did I set about trying to locate him, not to harm him but in order we could work on a way of solving this problem together and I'm hoping that is what is achieved by this meeting."

"Mr President no disrespect to you but I have already trusted one Politian and look at me now. I need to go to hospital for treatment later today, so why should I trust you or anyone in this room for that matter?"

"Matthew let all of us agree that while the past is tragic and nobody can deny that, today's meeting is all about how we can get this treatment into the open and start saving lives from this point onwards and we will work together to achieve that with no more threats of releasing this information and no more violence, do you agree?"

"Yes I do sir."

"Good and once we've done that, we will let the politicians and spin doctors cope with what's happened in the past shall we?"

"I'll be happy with that Sir," replied Matthew.

"Good and do you all agree with that?" The President asked.

They all replied in unison, "Yes we do Sir."

"Then let's get on with it shall we?"

"Matthew before we can proceed with anything, we do need to get the views of Dr Cooper." "Do you agree?"

"Yes I do Sir."

"So could you tell us where he is then?"

"No I'm sorry I can't but I will speak to him though to see if he agrees and I'm sure he will."

Matthew sat there thinking of his time in primary school when his form teacher, Mr Lambert said Michelin, you're a lazy stupid waste of space who will never achieve anything in his life and you're just taking the place of someone who deserves the opportunity that you're wasting. No doubt you'll be emptying my trash bins one day. Matthew also recalled what he said to him at the time, well if I do I hope you give a generous tip at Christmas. What a shame Lambert can't see him now, negotiating with the two most powerful men in the world. *Up yours Lambert*!

The President then said. "Don't take this the wrong way Matthew but I've heard some people referring to you as a drunken womanising manipulative idiot and that is who I expected to meet today. I have to say, I see in front of me a very loyal and trustworthy person, who just wants to do the right thing, without expecting any reward or personal gain, from his actions."

"Mr President I thank you for your kind words but I have to say that to some part you are wrong, as I do want some personal gain and that is to be given the treatment and return to the lifestyle I once had leading up to my stroke and I don't want anyone else to lose a loved one for no reason."

"That's understandable Matthew, so when can we expect you to contact Dr Cooper?"

"As soon I return from the hospital Sir."

"OK Matthew as far as I'm concerned, I've finished talking to you for now and as long as nobody else wants to ask you anything, I think you should go there right now, then we can resume as soon as you get agreement from Dr Cooper, let's say provisionally this time tomorrow shall we?"

Matthew left the room and the President said to the rest of the attendees, "Normally I wouldn't respond to threat's or blackmail but It's not like we're dealing with terrorist's are we, we are trying to help improve the life of people who are suffering, so as far as I'm concerned we need to do everything we can to help them with this treatment, as I still see Matthew as a very dangerous individual and while this thing is kept secret we will have no control over the outcome and I believe his threat."

"I do myself," replied the PM "Mr President I don't see this as a black mail situation but as a negotiation, so it would be both foolish and irresponsible, if we don't agree to work with them on their terms."

The President said, "I think that for security reasons we need to refer to this in future as the Miracle project," the video conference ended, leaving the UK group mumbling between themselves, the initial murmuring's were of approval. That is until Janette Kelly the health and social security secretary said, "Prime minister, may I just say something for the record?"

"Yes of course you may, Janette, what is it?"

"I have just done a quick mental calculation about what this could mean to the Health and Social security budget, however I would need to talk to the treasury and likewise I also need to confirm the number of people that could be affected by this should it go ahead."

"OK, Janette, tell us what you mean."

"Prime minister, if you were to take into account the cost of medication and social care, that may no longer be required and also disability living allowance payments, across the various illnesses, that this treatment claims it can reverse and I have only included in my quick calculation, stroke, diabetes and MS, the cost saving could be large enough to wipe out the national debt, if you were to include other ailments such as renal, heart, liver failure, paralysis, sight complaints, cerebral palsy and downs, the list is never ending according to Matthew."

"Carry on, Janette."

"We could be looking at saving Trillions of pounds over a period of time."

"What time scale would you estimate that to be Janette?" asked the PM.

"I'm sorry, Prime Minister, I couldn't say, we would need to call a cabinet meeting and assess which departments would be affected by the treatment, however the initial saving would be a year on year saving."

The PM said "Well it has to be a no brainer then."

Janette came back, "I'm sorry Prime Minister but it's not all good news."

"Why? Janette it seems like good news to me."

"I'm sorry Prime Minister, we need to consider the reverse side to the financial savings and I think you may agree that they could outweigh any financial saving that could be made."

"Go ahead Jeannette."

"I'm sorry Prime Minister I should have given you these details before the possible financial savings."

"Carry on Janette what are they?"

"There are over 1.5 million people of working age in the UK who currently receive disabled living allowance, the largest savings involving this group, would be achieved, by them coming off that benefit, as they would no longer be classed as disabled and therefore not qualify for that benefit any longer."

Malcolm Collins the Deputy PM, interrupted and said "Surely that's got to be a good thing, as we will have fewer disable people in the UK."

"Yes we would but these people would still be entitled to claim benefit and the only benefit available would be unemployment benefit or the dole and they can only receive that by signing on the unemployment register which would mean overnight we would have a further 1.5 million people added to the unemployment register."

Following this bombshell, the collective views turned from being pro the treatment to against, as the Deputy PM said, "Hang on let's think about this realistically, by treating these people we have now established there are no financial savings and if we treat them it will mean that politically we have a disaster on our hands, with the unemployment statistics increasing by that amount and no government could hope to survive if 1.5 million people are added to the unemployment statistics overnight."

Janette said "Surely we have a moral responsibility as a health service to try to provide the best treatment possible."

the Deputy PM said, "Come on Janette what Utopian world do you live in, there will be no benefit to us by overcoming disability if it politically affects our chances of winning the next election, we promised we would create jobs and reduce the unemployment levels and now you're saying overnight we will increase them by 1.5 million, our main responsibility has to be to the people who voted for us, enabling us to win the last election and to try to and attract the people who we hope will vote for us next time."

He continued, "If we announce the unemployment figures have risen by 1.5 million overnight, we will lose more votes than we gain, even if we eliminate some illnesses that to the most part only affect the old anyway."

Peter Pattern, the press officer, couldn't believe what he had just heard the Deputy PM say and while it wasn't his place, he felt he couldn't let him get away with it," Deputy PM if you think about it 1.5 million are people of working age, it's not just old people that these conditions affect, it's people of all ages, so in addition to the numbers Janette gave us there are probably double that number if you include the people who don't come into the working age bracket, OK some may be too young to vote but the vast majority will be over 65 and should be able to vote and don't forget the many parents and family members, of those who return to a normal life, who have a vote and could well vote for a party who introduced this treatment and those numbers are incalculable, so I think your being a bit short sighted by adopting the attitude you have."

The Deputy PM replied. "OK there may be more than 1.5 million, of course the over 65s can vote but what if all these people you've mentioned don't vote for us, we will have gained nothing, it is far too much of a gamble as far as I'm concerned."

He continued with his, objections, "If we don't allow this treatment to be used, we risk nothing. OK we save nothing but we won't have to cope with the reaction of the other parties, who would love to see that sort of rise in the unemployed."

Peter responded "But we deprive these people the right of returning to a normal life which we know they could have."

"Yes I know but we don't inflate the unemployment statistics and in my mind refusing this treatment to go ahead would be the lesser of the two evils, so I suggest that by doing nothing we reduce the risk of losing votes," and don't unnecessarily jeopardise our chances of being re-elected."

Even more disgusted by what he had just heard Malcolm Collins, say. Peter said "could someone confirm I just heard the Deputy Prime Minister suggest he thinks it would be better to keep people disabled and even let people die, just to keep this government in power than to provide the electorate with the level of medication and independence they deserve?"

"Come on now Peter, don't twist my words you know I didn't say that."

"No not in so many words you didn't but by implication you did. Should that be added to our next manifesto? Vote for our party and we guarantee that you will never lose your disabled living allowance and as a sub text *because we will do everything within our power to refuse you the treatment you require to regain your dignity and independence but we will also keep the unemployment numbers from rising."*

Peter could see the anger surfacing in Malcolm but couldn't hold his tongue.

"Can't you think about what's right for the people of the UK rather than yourselves for once?"

The PM said "that was a very noble speech Peter and very commendable, however the one thing that you seem to have forgotten is your employed by this government and as such I expect and demand your loyalty and I'm sure due to the very high salary you're paid, you should be able to come up with some kind of spin in your press release that will make us come out of this with some credit."

"OK Prime minister, how about this for a spin, if you remove the support you promised to give to President Peterson, you're out on a limb. The US are going to support Dr Cooper and Matthew with or without your backing and when they do you will have no alternative other than to allow the treatment to be used in the UK, forcing you to adopt the treatment, without you having any choice, so would you prefer to be given some credit for this treatment being developed, or just be considered as one of the many other countries that have been put in the shadow of the US as Peterson takes all the credit. Forget the unemployment numbers Prime Minister and come up with an alternative means of paying these people other than unemployment benefit. The other parties will gain no ground by objecting to a new benefit, who would object to the obvious improvement in people's wellbeing and independence, not to mention the savings you will still make in social care and ongoing medication costs."

"OK Peter I understand what you're saying but what about the objections from the pharmaceutical companies about the reduction in drugs sales, which we use to treat these conditions and their subsequent loss of profits?"

"With respect Prime minister is it you, or the pharmaceutical companies who run this country?"

"OK Peter you have a fair point but I will have to discuss this with the cabinet as it's not only the reduction in profits of these companies, the larger implication is the reduction in tax revenue, which is essential to the nation's budget. Malcolm can you contact my secretary and ask her to contact all cabinet ministers and tell them there is an emergency cabinet meeting called tonight and I expect everyone to attend without exception and to be here at number ten, by 7 p.m.?"

Matthew in the meantime was being transported to hospital by limousine, with two police outriders and accompanied by two of the biggest, ugliest and meanest looking bodyguards he had ever seen.

On arrival at the hospital, Matthew was treated as a VIP and rushed straight through the waiting room and into a cubicle, where he was examined by a Doctor and two nurses who removed the soiled bandages. The Doctor couldn't believe what he was looking at and enquired, "Who the hell has done this to you?"

"That's a long story don't ask."

"OK I won't but we do need to get this thing cleaned up and properly stitched, the Doctor gave instructions to the nurses, to remove the cotton stitches and clean the wound, he said, "This is going to be quite painful I'm afraid but if we don't do something I dread to think how bad an infection you could get, even gangrene could set in, which could cause a bit of problem, as unlike a leg or an arm we can't successfully cut your head off, with any guarantee of you making a full recovery."

Matthew started to laugh.

The youngest of the nurses, a tall red head held Matthew's hand and said, "At least you've still got a sense of humour."

"Look love what I've been through these last few days having my head cut off wouldn't be the worst of options. Hey is there any chance of some aesthetic to kill some of the pain?" he asked

The second nurse called the Doctor back in, "I think you should take a look at this Doctor there are some maggots under the flesh."

The Doctor said "I'm sorry Matthew this is a lot worse than I first feared, we need to take you through to surgery."

Still keeping his sense of humour Matthew said "Why, you're not cutting my head off are you?"

"Not yet."

"Well if you do is there any way you could transfer it to a body that can at least use all its arms and legs and with a few less pounds?"

The red headed nurse said "At least you didn't ask to have one that's hung like a horse."

"Why would I want to down size in that department?"

"Oh is that right?"

"Yes it is and if you're a good girl, I might just let you find out one day."

"I may just take you up on that then."

"Right if you write down your number and name for me we'll sort something out."

"Why do you want me to write it down, will you not remember my name?"

"With luck maybe not one day."

"What do you mean by that?"

"Nothing really it's just that after my operation, I may not be able to remember anything once I come around, that's if I do come around." Matthew was always scared of having a general anaesthetic.

"Don't be silly of course you'll come around. OK I'll write it on a note and put it inside your jacket pocket."

"Good and I'll arrange for us to meet up when I'm feeling a bit better."

"Good and don't make it too long."

"I won't I promise."

On his way to theatre Matthew was told he would have to be admitted overnight following his general anaesthetic, the Doctor informed his minders, who immediately contacted number ten and they were instructed to stay by his side all night and then bring him straight back to number ten the following morning and were instructed by Wilfred Morgan should anybody try to force their way into Matthews room, that they should take whatever action was deemed appropriate to protect him, he then asked "Do you understand by what, whatever action appropriate means?"

"Yes we do sir."

When Matthew arrived back at Number 10, the mood had seemed to change from the previous day.

The cabinet meeting had agreed to support the treatment but only because of what Peter Pattern had said about Peterson taking all the credit and having it forced on the UK anyway. Although most of the ministers in private if they were honest, would have ditched the treatment, as for them the embarrassment of the unemployment statistics rising by 1.5 million, was more important than looking after the wellbeing of the people and just like most politicians, saving their own skins was more important than doing the right thing. In the meantime Matthew emailed Mark, who agreed to the meeting and left Matthew to make the arrangements.

He informed the PM who in turn informed the President who insisted that the meeting should take place in Washington, so the US medical team could be present. Matthew asked the PM if he and Mark could meet in private beforehand and agree their strategy.

The PM suggested to the President "I think it would be a good idea for the pair of us to meet before as well."

Peterson replied "I have a very tight schedule, so I don't know if I could meet you beforehand."

The PM replied "Mr President I believed Matthew's threat that we have four weeks so we need to move quickly."

Stupidly the President protested, "Yes I know but I just don't know how I can fit it in."

The PM said "we are both at the state banquette at Buckingham palace in a couple of weeks so we could spend an hour or two talking about it, either before or after the banquet. Then once you fly back to Washington, we can arrange the meeting for a day or two after let's say the 29th of this month."

"That's fine with me but I'll just have to contact a couple of people and make sure they have a free diary that day."

"OK I will speak to Matthew to check that day is OK for the both of them and I'll get back to you later today."

The PM told Matthew the meeting was to be held in Washington, on the 29th and asked him if he could let Dr Cooper know for him to make sure he was there on that date and that his office would make arrangements for Matthew's flight to Washington.

"No way," Matthew said.

"Sorry," replied the PM "What do you mean by that?"

"I mean there is no way, am I getting on a plane, that you've arranged for me to fly on."

"Why not?" asked the PM

Matthew replied "because some planes have been known to blow up midway across the Atlantic that's why."

"Don't be foolish Matthew, are you suggesting that I'm going to put you on a plane and then arrange for it to be blown up?"

"That's right I am."

"Come on Matthew, I thought you had started to trust us."

"I would prefer to be trapped in a cage with a starving tiger and trust that not to eat me than to trust you."

"Now you're just being childish, so how will you manage to get to Washington?"

"I'm prepared to fly there but only if the President in sitting next to me on the same flight."

"Matthew the President only ever flies on Air Force One."

"That's OK by me I'm sure there'll be plenty of spare seats on that."

"Matthew there is no way you will be allowed to fly on Air Force One."

"OK but there's no way I will be meeting anyone in Washington then."

"Come on Matthew, be reasonable."

"Bollocks to reasonable and bollocks to you and your meeting as well."

"Right I'll try and see what I can do." The PM left Matthew and re-entered his office, the President's face was already on the screen.

"Good afternoon gentlemen," the PM said to the team gathered in the Whitehouse.

"Good afternoon Prime Minister and all you other ladies and Gentlemen," replied Peterson. "Do we have the meeting arranged Prime Minister?"

"We do have a slight problem Mr President."

"OK, what's that?"

"Matthew is still as paranoid as ever, he is saying that he will not fly to Washington unless the President is on the same plane as he is."

David Prendergast shouted "Just who does this limey asshole think he's dealing with, who's he to tell us what he will do and won't do?"

Malcolm Collins didn't see eye to eye with David Prendergast, from the moment they first met, the pair had locked horns, Malcolm had questioned David's commitment to dealing with terrorists, he accused him of double standards, based on David's previous role as Mayor of New York, when he openly encouraged the Irish American population to raise funds for the IRA prolonging the conflict in Northern Ireland and contributing the deaths of ordinary British troops and civilians, plus David's criticism of the UK's policy of internment without trial of hundreds of Irish people, which he now found ironic, when years later David Prendergast was instrumental in introducing the same policy at Guantanamo Bay during the USA's war on terror, even though Malcolm Collin's supported the policy, he still found David Prendergast someone who irritated him and whenever he heard the man speak he thought that David he had been promoted way above his ability, in line with the Peter principle[5] and whenever they found themselves in each other's company, they never missed the opportunity to wind each other up and to lock horns with one another and this occasion was going to be no different, Malcolm immediately took exception to David's comment and said.

"Look Prendergast for once, in your life why don't you try to be professional!"

"I didn't think it would be long before you opened your big mouth Collins. I asked you a question, who does this limey ass hole think he is. So is there any chance you could contribute something useful to a meeting for once by at least answering me?"

Malcolm Collins replied, "He's a British citizen that's who he is."

"So what's that, got to do with it Collins?"

"He's our guy and we will look after him and if you want him to save your incompetent Yankee ass, I think you need to keep your big mouth shut. So if the only way our guy will come to your country is by making sure you murdering bastards don't kill him on the way there, is by the President being with him to keep him safe, that's what's going to have to happen and that's down to you evil murdering bastards in the first place."

"How do you work that one out Collins?"

"Have you seen the state of his head after your murdering thugs got hold of him?"

"So, Prendergast, if the only option is the President's on the same plane that's your choice, take it or leave it."

---

[5] The Peter Principle is a theory suggested by Laurence J Peter in a humorous book, The Peter Principle: why things go wrong, he co-authored the book with Raymond Hull in 1969, suggesting that in most large organisation, people are promoted until they reach their own position of incompetence.

David replied, "The President only ever flies on Air Force One."

"It looks like he's going to have a passenger then doesn't it," replied Malcolm.

"Are you crazy there's no way that's going to happen, the limey shit house won't by flying on Air Force One, It's not a fucking taxi service you know."

"If that's the case and if I was you Prendergast, I would spend the rest of the evening writing a new resume, as there's only one way you're going to keep those incompetent Yankee sass's in the luxury of the White house and that's with the help of our man."

"Who are you calling incompetent, why don't you let your organ grinder say what he feels?"

"Hang on Prendergast I'm the Deputy PM."

"Exactly that's what you are. The Deputy and looking around both rooms you're the only person who has the word Deputy before his title, so I think you should take your rightful place and just listen to the people who out rank you."

This was only the beginning of them trading insults.

"That's enough of that David" said the President.

Malcolm Collins said "so what don't you understand about 28 days because of the proposed meeting date, we will already be 14 days into the 28, so unless you can come up with an alternative suggestion that Matthew will accept, it looks like, if our man isn't going to be blowing your election campaign, he's going to have white house luggage labels on his suit case's, your choice Prendergast."

"Look you're not telling us what we've got to do Deputy, were the United States of America, nobody tells us what to do, we tell them, do you understand fat man?" the insults continued.

"Fuck off, big mouth," Replied Malcolm.

"Hey, you two, grow up will you," said an angry President Peterson. "David we seem to have no option, other than to arrange for Mr Michellin to be allowed to fly to Washington on Air Force One."

David's voice was raised, when he said.

"What the hell do you think you're doing, have you lost your mind? I'm not going to allow you to make a decision just like that. We need to consider the security implications and the reaction of congress if we turn Air Force One into a taxi service for some paranoid Limey."

"David I've made the decision, deal with it and I've just about had enough of your attitude today, so calm down and how dare you speak to me like that, now I want you to apologise to Mr Collins."

"There's no way I'm apologising to him and there is no way that limey coward is getting on Air Force One."

"David let me ask you a question, who is the President of the United States here?"

"Well you are I suppose."

"That's right I am and make sure you don't you ever forget that!"

"I'm sorry, sir; I just got a bit annoyed because of what the boy was saying."

"That's enough, David, I've already told you once and I won't tolerate your behaviour any longer. I think it's time you left this meeting."

"What you're sending me out of the meeting?"

"Yes I am."

"So how long, before you would like me to come back in?"

"David I don't want you to come back into the meeting. The meeting will continue without you and so will the miracle project, I want you to leave right now, before I call security and have you physically removed."

"OK I will," David Prendergast stood up, looking and feeling totally humiliated and thinking to himself as he walked out of the room, *you're not going to get away with this Peterson, this is one mistake you've made that* won't *go away.* On his way out he glanced back towards the screen on which he could see Malcolm Collins looking smug and smirking, however as much as he hated the man Malcolm did have some empathy with David Prendergast and a small degree of sympathy, although he would never admit it.

Malcolm Collins is a proud Lancastrian who was born into a working class North of England family he had been educated in the days before comprehensive schools were introduced to the education system and he was proud to have received an old secondary modern school education, believing that it gave him a better grounding in the practical requirements in life. He started work as a fifteen year old and trained as an electrician, leaving school without any academic qualifications but had gone on to college and night school, acquiring the qualifications he was proud to hold today. He had originally started his political career as a labour MP but he fell out and became disillusioned with his party and its anti-nuclear pacifist polices during the late seventies and early eighties, at a time when the cold war was in full swing but in spite of feeling he had no future in his party, he could have never contemplated walking across the floor of the house, as in those days, as he couldn't abide the Tories although he did have a secrete admiration for the Iron Lady, Maggie Thatcher, who had fought and won two major battles during her time as PM she had decided to take on and beat the unions, even though he had been a strong union supporter in his late teens and early twenties and had become a shop steward when he worked for Manchester council but even he was fed up with the way the unions were ruining the country as a result of all the strikes they kept calling causing. For Malcolm the one strike that broke the camel's back and for most other union supporters at the time was the miners' strike which all but crippled the country but ironically it was this strike that ultimately lead to the demise of the unions and he also admired the way she stood up to and wiped the arses of the Argies, over the Falkland Islands and how she put the Great back into Great Britain. While he would never describe himself as a Tory, he most definitely couldn't support the policies or the leadership of the Labour party of the day or in recent times. As much as he admired Mrs Thatcher, he couldn't agree with a lot of her policies and it was those polices that had stopped him from switching to the Tories in those days but he only wished that there was a PM of her calibre around today as no one pulled her strings, she was definitely her own man, so to speak!

He surprised everyone when he did eventually cross the floor of the house from being a back bench labour MP to become a front bench Tory MP he was accused by the left wing media of selling out but he didn't see it that way, his Own justification was he thought he could best beat the Tory right wing policies, by becoming the enemy within and he would argue he had done that to the most part.

The makeup of the guy if the truth be known was while he was comfortable in most people's company, he would much prefer to be sat at the side of the likes of Sir Alex Ferguson, the Manager of his beloved Manchester United soccer team, than sat with the Lord's, Ladies and Dignitaries, he often finds himself having dinner with at official functions. In private he was more of a Republican, than a monarchist but don't misjudge him. He was a passionate Brit and a patriotic Englishman, who had campaigned in the past to keep the UK a United Kingdom and argued passionately that Scotland, should remain a part of the union, he also argued that while the national anthem God save the Queen should remain as the anthem of Great Britain and the union flag should remain its standard, he passionately argued that like the Scots, Welsh and Irish, who all had their own anthems and flags, the English should make more use of their own anthem, and flag, Land of hope and glory and the George Cross respectively, on far more occasions than just the commonwealth games, he also believed that, ST Georges day should be a day of national celebration and patriotism in England and also a bank holiday and he became really angry when all those, Liberal namby pamby, welcome to the U.K with open arms brigade, argued that, that would be seen as being to nationalistic and racist, when he heard that, his Northern passion would cause his blood to boil and just as David Prendergast had been today, he had been asked to leave many a meeting in the past when his shop floor language, would get the better of him.

Take him or leave him, what you see is what you get. In him a better friend and ally you couldn't find, however, an enemy, make one of him and you have an enemy for life.

Chapter 6
Back in Manchester

As soon as Matthew arrived back in Manchester he phoned Andrea and arranged to meet her the following evening in the bar attached to the Portland hotel. He asked his brother if he could give him a lift into Manchester, Jim said "no problem but I want a word with you first." When Jim arrived he said. "Where have you been our kid? We've all been going frantic with worry again."

"Look, Jim, if I told you just wouldn't believe me."

"Why? Try me. We need to know what you've got yourself into because you've changed."

"OK, Jim, but by telling you what you want to know, I'm going to put both of us in a position I rather wouldn't want to."

"If you don't, you know I won't give in and just keep on at you until you do tell me."

"OK, but whatever I tell you, you've got to promise me you won't tell anyone anything."

"Just tell me will you Matt?"

"OK I will, but whoever it is who asks you, I've got to know you won't say anything to anyone." He continued "when I was in St Kitts something happened that was unbelievable and you can't even tell anyone where I've been especially that I've been to St Kitts."

"Why what have you done?"

"I've done nothing Jim, you're not going to believe me but I'm being hunted down by some people."

"Why what do they want with you?"

"They want to stop me releasing some information I have."

"Is it to do with the book your writing and being a journalist Matt?"

"Yes and no."

"Bollocks, what do you mean, yes and no?"

"Jim what I have, is information that could bring the governments of both the US and UK to their knees."

"Talking of knees, you've not uncovered another episode in the oral office have you, this time involving Peterson?"

"No it's much bigger than that, if I publish what I have, the whole of the western governments would prefer it if they had all been caught with their pants down in the oral office."

"Why what have you got?"

"Can you see my head?"

"Yes how did you, do that?"

"I've just had an emergency operation to save my life."

"What was wrong with you was it something terminal?"

"No I took a beating and I then needed to have it looked at."

"So who did it to you?"

"Now this is where your minds going to be blown apart, I was tortured by the CIA to get the information I have and that's why I don't want you involved as they could come after you."

Jim's concern for his brother was now overshadowed by his reluctance to take a beating, "Right our kid," he said, "I don't want to know anything but is this just a load of bull shit you're telling me."

"No it's not, it's true."

In spite of his own fears, Jim's curiosity and his concern for his brother's wellbeing, he forced himself to ask Matthew more questions, "So why would people like that be interested in anything you may have?"

"It's something that their governments haven't allowed to happen during the last ten years and if they had it would have changed all our lives and if I was to put it in a book or the papers they would be in bigger shit than anyone could ever imagine and it's not only the CIA that's after me, it's MI5 as well, plus the Israelis and others."

"Bollocks our kid I don't believe you."

"It's true, Jim, and now the CIA guys just want to protect me from being taken by others."

"Come, on our kid stop all this bull shit."

Matthew continued "Jim did you read anything in the paper about two guys found dead at Manchester Airport?"

"Yes I did."

"What was said?"

"Nothing other than one of the dead guys had his throat cut and the other had his neck broken and police are trying to find out who they were, and they are looking for three people, one with a limp and a bandage on his head and the other two spoke with American accents that's, all."

"Come on, our kid, how would you describe me to someone if I was meeting them somewhere for the first time today and who had no idea who I was?"

Jim thought for a minute and said, "I would probably say you had a walking stick and a bandage on your head."

"Fine now add to that who has just told you he had been tortured by two American agents. Come on, Inspector Colombo, how long would it take you to put two and two together?"

"You're talking bollocks, our kid."

"Am I?"

"Come on what would you have to do with it?"

"OK, our kid, the two guys were Israeli agents. The Mossad and they were trying to kill me and the two CIA guys saved me and killed them."

"So if you were at the airport where were you going, Matt?"

"I was on my way to a meeting with the PM and the President in Downing Street."

"I tell you what, it's no wonder your books are a big success because you tell a fucking good story."

"Fine you keep thinking that way at least it will stop you asking me questions. Yes you're right, Jim, it's just a plot from my latest book and I'm going to Washington in the next month to promote my book, so tell no one what I've told you, in case the story gets out and the book is spoilt."

"What are you up to now, Matt?"

"I'm meeting a stewardess I met on the way home from St Kitts, fit as a butcher's dog."

"Right where am I dropping you?"

"You're dropping me outside the Portland hotel."

"Then what?"

"A few drinks, a Chinese, a load of charm and then fingers crossed, it could be a good night."

"So what time shall I pick you up?"

"Can I ring you later Jim?"

"Yes, no problem and have a nice time, Matt."

"Cheers, our kid, but I'm hoping it's going to be a lot better than just nice."

Matthew entered the bar and Andrea was sat in a secluded corner, she saw him and asked him "What's happened to your head?"

"Nothing serious I just fell over and got an infection in the cut, so I had to spend a bit of time in hospital." He asked the waiter, "Could I have a Manhattan and whatever the lady wants please?"

Andrea asked him, "can you make that two Matthew and isn't this the Gay Village?"

"Yes it is but only on the outskirts."

"Do you spend a lot of time in the gay village?"

"No not much."

She said to him, "Am I going to have to keep my eyes on you?"

"No you don't have to worry about me in that way."

"Well two guys over there haven't taken their eyes off you, since you came in you know."

"Well they're only human. Sometimes these looks can be a bit of a burden and things like that don't interest me at all."

"I hope not because what I have planned for us tonight, we both need to be straight for."

He replied, "You don't have to worry about me, I'm as straight as they come."

"None the less I'm going to keep a tight hold of you."

"Good but we better get going as I've booked a table."

She said "I'm looking forward to this."

"I'm sure you'll enjoy it," they both left and crossed the road into China Town, "Manchester has the best Chinese food I've eaten anywhere I've ever been," Matthew said. They entered the restaurant and one of the waiters welcomed Matthew and said to him.

"Hello, Matthew, drinks?"

"Yes please."

"Your usual?"

"Yes please, but make it two will you," he replied.

Andrea said to him, "I see you're a celeb here."

"Not quite I wouldn't say that."

"You seem to be well known," they sat at a table and ordered some fantastic food, the waiter brought over a cheap bottle of champagne.

"On the house, Matthew," he said.

They had a good time and a great meal and when they had finished Matthew asked for the bill and made his way to the toilet and on his way out of the toilet a middle-aged guy bumped into him, he apologised and he spoke to Matthew in French, Matthew thought *That's strange; one thing you don't normally see in Manchester are the French,* the guy sat down with three other men and Matthew could hear them all speaking French.

He was keeping his eye on the time and thinking of Jim having to drive from his home, which would take about 20 minutes, Matthew asked Andrea "would you like a coffee and a brandy?"

She said "I would love one but I've got a bottle of brandy in my hotel bed room if you fancy coming back and sampling it with me?"

He said "Under normal circumstances, I would jump at the offer but I'm sorry I just can't tonight."

"Are you turning me down?"

"No not turning you down, I'm just taking a rain check, you see my brothers picking me up in a couple of minutes and I've promised to phone my agent in Washington, tonight at midnight and I can't miss doing it and all my notes are at home."

That's disappointing," she replied and added, "maybe some other time then and I've had fabulous time thanks for tonight."

"So you fancy meeting me again?" asked Matthew.

"I would love to."

"That's great, but I have to fly out of the country in the next few days."

"What back to St Kitts?"

"No the States; I've got some marketing to do and some book signing and an interview on the *Tonight* program. So when I'm back I'll ring you and rather than going out, how about I cook you something at my house?"

She said to him, "A man of many talents not only a Journalist and an Author but a local celeb and now a chef what else are you expert at?"

"Well there's one thing you've still to sample."

"I was hoping to do that tonight, but I'll just have to wait now until after our meal."

"It will be worth the wait I promise."

"It better had be as I'm a very greedy girl and I always want seconds."

"Don't worry you will most probably get thirds, fourths, and fifths, as well."

"Wow Marathon man, is there no end to your talents?"

"Sadly I can't tap dance or juggle any longer."

She laughed.

"Look I'm sorry Jim's here, I will have to go," he told her.

"OK so kiss me then."

Which he did while standing outside the restaurant, afterwards he climbed into Jim's car and as he looked back at Andrea he noticed the four French guys running to get into two cars.

Jim said, "You've done well for yourself there, our kid."

"Just wait till you see the real thing the Rusky, she is something special."

Jim pulled out and while Matthew was looking back, he noticed two cars pull out behind them, he thought *oh shit*.

He said to Jim, "Look, our kid, don't worry about this but I think were being followed."

"*WHAT?*" Was Jim's, reply.

Matthew said "just keep going, don't stop for anything, red light's, nothing."

"Who is it?" asked Jim.

"It's probably just someone's husband or boyfriend, who has eventually caught up with me."

"Are you sure that it's not one of those so called agents who are looking for you?"

"I don't know at the moment but I think their French whoever they are, so I guess they could be."

"There you go again with all your bull shit, you know very well they're not fucking agents."

"I hope your right, our kid."

"Matt why are you doing you his to me? All these lies and games you're playing. I'm shitting myself that you're going to get yourself killed or something, I can no longer work out if you're lying or not. It's wrong to put me through this, making me worry; Matt, I think you should see a Doctor. You've changed, we never used to have any secrets; now I feel I no longer know you anymore what's going on, Matt, and I want the truth?"

"OK, Jim, everything I told you before was the truth, I am being hunted down, it wasn't just a plot from my book and I am working with the President of the US and the UK Prime minister."

"Matt, don't start that bull shit again."

"Jim, what the fuck will it take, for you to believe me one way or the other?"

Jim replied, "So who is it that's following us then."

"I don't know, but they can't catch us whoever they are."

"OK bull shitter, where are the guys who are supposed to be looking after you?"

"I don't know" Matt replied.

Jim said, "Matt since you started writing you've become engulfed in a world of fantasy, as opposed to reality, not knowing any longer the difference between the two worlds."

"Since when did you graduate as a psychologist our kid?" Matthew asked.

"Around about the time you became double O six and seven eight's."

"Jim I'm no different than I've always been."

"Yes I've forgotten, you've always mixed with world leaders and had agents following you and trying to kill you, haven't you?"

"Maybe not agents but Husband's and boyfriend's, yes."

"Are these people behind us trying to kill you?"

"Yes probably! Unless I give them the information their after."

"Oh great, so where are your minders?"

"They won't be too far away."

Jim still not fully convinced if Matthew was telling the truth, was still worried about who may be following them, as husbands or boyfriends with baseball bats, can still do you a lot of damage. "Matt if this isn't bullshit your minders are not in this car, so as far as I'm concerned their too far away for my liking, can't you just phone them?"

"Jim, just try to lose them will you?"

"I'm trying."

"Well stop driving like a Fanny and try harder will you, just don't let them catch up with us and head home as fast as you can."

Jim, never the greatest driver, at the best of times was now speeding through the traffic, horns blaring out from the cars on either side of the road, the ones he was cutting up on his side of the road and the ones he was causing to swerve on the opposite side of the road. Matthew looked over his shoulder and noticed they were getting closer. "Jim, take the side streets, try to lose them. I was told to expect something like this and if so just head towards home and the CIA will meet me there."

"Told to expect what? Cars chasing you and people trying to kill you?"

"Yes."

"Matt, you can't live like this, being chased by people trying to kill you."

"Don't worry, Jim, after I've been to Washington, everything will be OK I promises. Take the side streets and just lose them."

They pulled off the main drag and into a side street and ran over a push bike that had been left in the middle of the road, smashing the front and the underneath of Jim's car, his car was his pride and joy and he looked annoyed, Matt said, "forget about that, just put your foot down and lose them."

Jim was now even more pissed off with Matt, for breaking his car.

Jim looked through his rear view mirror and noticed the passenger in the car directly behind them was leaning through the passenger side window and he had a gun in his hand, he screamed, "Shit, Matt, they're shooting at us!"

"Jim, don't worry, just try to lose them."

Jim said, "Don't worry are you for real, we're being shot at while driving through the streets of Harpurhey[6]."

"No difference there then, just an everyday occurrence around here," the very next moment the rear window of Jim's car exploded as a bullet came through and lodged in the sun visor just above Jim's head.

"Matt, do something for fuck's sake will you?"

Matthew opened his wallet and took out the card that Giovanni had given him with his phone number on to call if he needed him; well he did now so Matthew rang him.

---

[6] Harpurhey is a suburb of Manchester, which in recent times has become known for its gun crime.

Gio answered the phone, Matthew said, "I'm in the shit here," he told Gio what was happening.

Giovanni said, "Just keep calm, do you remember the industrial estate where we took you?"

"How could I ever, forget?"

"Just head there and we'll be there in ten minutes, how many of them are there?"

"Four I think in two cars."

"OK see you soon, try to lose them on the way."

"That's what we're trying to do."

"Who was that?" asked Jim.

"That was one of my minders."

"So what are they doing?"

"We need to meet them on the way to Oldham."

"Where, I'll put it in my sat nav?"

"Fuck the sat nav, just head towards Oldham."

"Tell me where, will you?"

"Just keep going as fast as you can and lose them."

"If you don't promise me you're going to get this thing sorted, I'm going to stop the car right now and have a word with these guys."

"Don't be a fucking knob, Jim, your days in the army cadets and Special Forces boy scouts equipped you for this type of thing did they, look arsehole if you do stop, we'll both soon be together in the same hole in the ground. Jim I'll get it sorted trust me."

Then another bullet hit the wing mirror on Jim's side of the car.

"Take the next left, now right, then second left, third right, then the third left, are they still with us?"

"One of them is."

"Which one's still with us?"

"I don't know."

Then the two guys in the second car, started to shoot at them but this time it was an automatic weapon they were using, as three bullets hit the car in quick succession, all Jim said was, "Well that's completely fucked up my no claim's bonus!"

"OK now take the next left."

"Try to tell me sooner will you!"

Jim turned the wheel so late and hard they almost went round the corner sideways but it did the trick the second car went straight past "Now next right, then second left, then first right and we're there."

They pulled into the estate.

Matthew said, "Oh shit, they're not here."

"That's good isn't it, we've lost them."

"No not them, my friends," replied Matthew.

"So you're saying we've got no help."

"Just pull behind that skip, Jim, and hide the car," which de did but owing to Jim being a rubbish driver, he kept manoeuvring backwards and forwards, before it was hidden. Matthew shouted, "For fuck's sake just stop the fucking car, will you? Well done we can't be seen from the road now. Great job of driving our kid, I'll never say you're a shit driver again but next time you pick me up, can you just go back to being how shit you normally are."

"Shut up, dick head," replied Jim.

Matthew said, "Let's get out of the car and hide behind the unit."

"I've got a better idea," said Jim.

"What's that?"

"Phone the police, that's what," replied Jim.

"No way, Jim, we can't do that."

"Why not, knob head?"

"Jim, just get out of the car will you," as they did, there was a screech of tyres as a car sped onto the estate.

"Oh shit!" cried Jim.

"Don't worry, Jim, it's the goodies[7]," replied Matthew.

Jim said, fucking Bill Oddie, Graham Garner and Tim Brooke Taylor's no good to us!

"No dick head my mates the good guys," the car screeched to a halt outside the door of the unit, both agents jumped out and it was Giovanni who shouted, "Matthew where are you?"

"Here behind the skip."

"Where are they?" asked Gio.

"I think we lost them."

Then two cars drove slowly past the estate. It was now getting dark, Dolff with gun in hand pointing at Jim said, "Who's this then?"

"It's my brother."

"So how much does he know?"

"Not much more than someone's just been trying to kill us, so I think he suspects something is going on."

"Let's get inside where it's safer," said Dolff.

They all went into the office.

Giovanni turned on the lights. Matthew said "what are you doing? They'll find us."

---

[7] *The Goodies* was a 1970s TV comedy show in the UK staring Bill Oddie, Graham Garner and Tim Brook Taylor.

"That's what we want," said Dolff.

"Oh shit! Why?" asked Jim.

Dolff said, "We need to know who they are that's why."

"I don't need to know," replied Jim, he then said, "but I know what I do need to know."

"What's that?"

"Where's the toilet?" replied Jim.

Dolf said, "I'll take you."

"Good but don't leave me alone will you."

"No I'll stay with you until you're finished."

There was a staircase at the side of the toilet leading to, a mezzanine floor. Jim went into the cubicle. Dolff stayed in the warehouse, where there were rows and rows of high racking stacked with boxes and palettes full of goods, which made it ideal to conceal yourself.

Dolf stepped into the toilet area and checked that Jim was still in the cubicle, as Dolf re-entered the warehouse the front door of the unit suddenly burst open with a bang. Giovanni took two guns from his coat pocket and gave Matthew one, "ever used on of these before?"

"No never."

"Just point it and pull the trigger, don't act like Clint Eastwood, just sit there and shoot anyone who tries to get you and if anything happens to both me and Dolf, just put it to the side of your head and pull the trigger."

"What about Jim?"

"Just shoot the Mother fucker, either way."

Then two of the guys ran into the warehouse, both carrying automatic hand guns, they had no idea the CIA were already here waiting for them.

One of them went into the racking area, while the other went upstairs to the next floor, the one in the racking area was slowly popping his head around each rack looking for someone and while he was doing so, Dolf was stealthily trying to get into the perfect position to deal with him. As the guy was looking down the racks, Jim came out of the toilets, the guy turned and raised his gun, Jim froze to the spot but before he could fire at Jim, Dolf shot him twice in the head, he fell onto the floor. Jim could see the guy's head sticking out of the aisle, blood spurting from the wounds to his head and his brains splattered all over the floor. Jim turned around and went straight back into the toilet, the guy upstairs came down and saw his mate and started to shoot his automatic gun indiscriminately down each racking aisle hoping to hit anyone down there, with bullets ricocheting off the metal racking Dolf needed to be careful not to be hit by any wayward bullet. Gio appeared behind the guy and plunged a commando knife into his back; the guy just gurgled and fell to the floor. Dolf went towards him and bent down at the side of him and stabbed him over and over again, he then took his ID from his pocket and put it in his own.

Giovanni said to Dolff, "Is that all of them?"

"I don't know, we got two but didn't Matthew say he thought there were four of them?" At that time Jim came out of the toilet, once the door opened Dolf got off a shot in his direction but fortunately he missed.

Giovanni shouted, "Look asshole either stay in there and finish your shit, or go into the office with Matthew." Jim went back into the toilet just as the depot door burst open and two more guys ran in carrying semi-automatic weapons, one had a hand gun the other had a sub machine gun, both the CIA guys saw them at the same time. One of the new guys ran down the first isle and disappeared. The other was immediately shot in the head by Giovanni. The next thing you heard was Jim shouting, "Is it all right to come out yet?" The fourth guy went towards the toilet just as Dolf was about to jump on him from the side of a large crate. Dolf took out his gun to shoot him in the back, he aimed pulled the trigger but he was out of bullets, the click alerted the forth guy, so he spun around to see where it had come from, he then started to empty the magazine of his semi-automatic machine gun into the area he thought he had heard the noise come from but in doing so he failed to notice Giovanni closing in behind him. Gio took out his commando knife grabbed him by the hair and slit his throat so hard it nearly decapitated him.

Just then Jim came out of the toilet once again. Giovanni dropped the body at the feet of Jim, who ran back into the toilet. Giovanni and Dolf then went into the office to make sure Matthew was OK. Matthew said, "Is our kid OK?"

"Yes he is and he won't have to worry about being constipated for a while."

Jim walked into the office his face was as white as a sheet and asked, "Is there any more toilet paper?"

Dolff said, "Are you for fucking real or what?"

Jim replied, "What the fuck was that all about?"

Giovanni replied, "Probably the best enema you've ever had, or likely to have!"

"Who were they?" asked Matthew.

Dolf replied, "**DGSE,** General Directorate of external security, in other words the French secret service."

"Are we OK now?" Matthew asked.

For the time being," Dolf replied.

Jim said, "Hang on what's happening, our kid. The French Secrete Service, why are they after you?"

"Just to stop me publishing the information I have, or to stop me giving it to another publisher!"

"So, who are these two then, Mills and fucking Boon[8] I suppose," referring to Dolf and Gio.

"No we're CIA," replied Gio.

"Oh shit, Matt, are these your two friends?"

"Yes they are."

"So you were telling me the truth before."

"OK I was but keep quiet about it Jim."

"Matt you've got to get yourself out of whatever this thing is!"

"Jim I told you I was meeting the President, so they've been sent over to check me out and make sure I get there safely."

"OK but they've just killed four people and what happens when this place opens tomorrow and they find dead bodies all over the place and worse still no toilet paper?"

"Giovanni said "Don't worry buddy we own this place."

Jim said "Who do; the CIA?"

"Yes so within the hour it will look like they were never even born."

"Look Matt enough is enough, I want to know how far this thing is going and that you're going to be safe and how many more Nutter's are going to come after you?"

"Once I've met the President and briefed him I'm going to be fine, so stop going on will you."

Gio said, "Look Jim he will have round the clock protection, he will be as safe as the President himself."

---

[8] Mills and Boon is a publishing company specialising in romance.

Jim said, "What you mean just as safe as Lincoln, McKinley, Garfield, Kennedy and even Ronnie Regan, who was shot in front of his own secret service guys?"

Gio said, "Look Jim, I'm sure you're worried but there's no need to be he will come to no harm I promise you."

"He better hadn't and what about my car?"

"What do you mean?"

"I mean who's, going to pay for the damage to it?"

"Don't worry, we'll sort it out."

"It better be as good as it was," said Jim.

Gio took Matthew, to one side and whispered, "We will get him a brand new one, what do you think he would like?"

"Something with at least the same spec, maybe a brand new one of the one he's got and red."

"So talk to him, about whatever he wants and well get it for him."

Matthew asked, "Why would you do that?"

"We've then got him on the pay role and we can control him, we will also arrange a visit for him and his family to go anywhere in the world they want."

Matthew went back to talk to Jim, "Look everything you've seen or heard today our kid, don't mention it to anyone, firstly they won't believe you, secondly you'll just make yourself, Betty and Andy a target, so nothing happened today, OK!"

"OK but what do I say about the car to Betty?"

"I'm sure you'll come up with something our kid.," We'll give you a lift home and the next time I see you is when I'm home from Washington."

"Well make sure you keep safe Matt."

"I will and you make sure you keep quiet our kid."

"I will but what about my car?"

"These guys are going to sort it next week, in fact they'll get you a new car and anything you want."

"What do you mean?"

"Either a brand new one of what you've already got, or whatever you want."

"You mean anything?"

"Yes anything."

"You mean I could have a five series Bema or a Lexus?"

"Yes I do."

"So will they get me anything that I want?"

"How many more times our kid, for fuck sake yes anything you want."

"OK but it better be red and top of the range."

"So which one do you want?"

Jim thought for a second and said, "Go on a Bema then."

Matt thought, *fucking asshole, he could have gone for a, Bentley, or a Ferrari and he's chose a BMW,* "Where have you ever wanted to go in the world our kid?"

"I've always fancied Hong Kong."

Matthew was surprised he didn't say Skegness or somewhere like that, "Right you're going.

"I'm going to Hong Kong why?"

"They feel bad about what you've been put through today and it's just by way of a thank you."

"What do you mean a thank you?"

"For getting me here safely, so a Bema and Hong Kong you fancy it then, are you sure you wouldn't want a bit more time to think it through?"

"No I'm fine but only if it's five star accommodation, first class flights and all inclusive."

"You're a cheeky bastard our kid, I'll make sure they know what you want."

"Great and Hong Kong does it include Betty and Andy?"

"Course it does."

"Does it have to?" Jim was only joking.

"Take care, Matt."

"You as well our, kid."

That was it, Jim was happy and so was Matthew.

Chapter 7
The Best Taxi Ride Ever

Matthew was once again picked up by Gio and Dolf and transported to Manchester Airport, from where he was to be flown by private jet to London, with his new stewardess friend looking after him, this time they were to land at Heathrow airport, for him to catch his flight to Washington on board Air Force One.

Prior to entering the Presidential aircraft, Matthew was treated almost as a terror suspect, even though David Prendergast had conceded to Petersons demands, the CIA chief wasn't going to make this easy or enjoyable for Matthew.

Matthew was subjected to the humiliation of a strip search and even worse a cavity search. When he did eventually board the aircraft, he was blown away by its splendour. He thought the private jets he had been flying on were luxurious but by comparison this was palatial. He met the President for the first time face to face and he was invited to join him at his private table, also at the table was a tall man, who turned out to be a Professor of psychology from Harvard University. They chatted about day to day things, like the state of the British weather, Manchester, the economy, etc. The stewardess brought a jug of Manhattan's to the table and three glasses, Matthew being Matthew was on her like a shot trying to get her to meet him for a drink that night in Washington, he was also allowed to smoke. He commented to the professor, "I didn't expect that you would be able to smoke on board."

"You can do almost anything you like on here within reason."

Matthew said, "Does that also include the stewardess?"

The professor replied "I hope not."

Matthew said, "Saving her for yourself then?"

The professor replied "I wouldn't have thought that would be acceptable somehow."

"Why not?" asked Matthew, "I'm sure the President wouldn't mind accommodating you."

"Well you see she is my daughter after all."

Foot in mouth once again, Matthew said he was sorry and enquired would his new friend fancy sharing another jug of Manhattan before take-off. He asked the President if that would be OK?

The President replied, "Of course it will."

Matthew called the professors daughter over and asked her to bring another jug, which she did and even before the aircraft had taxied to its starting position the second jug was empty, with Matthew having by far the lion's share of both jugs.

"You seem very thirsty Mr Michellin," the professor said.

"Just a nervous flyer," replied Matthew, "as the President can vouch."

"There's no need to worry about that, you're on the safest aircraft in the world."

"That's easy to say, I'll only begin to think that way after a few more jugs of this or when we're safely on the runway in one piece in Washington."

The professor said to his daughter, "Could we have another one of these? I think you best keep them coming all through the flight."

"I'm sorry but we're just about to take off but as soon as we have I'll bring you one over."

Matthew looked at her and the professor and thought *what a shame* but he was still determined to get her number before he left the plane.

The professor said to Matthew, "No more alcohol for you this week."

"Why not?" replied Matthew.

"I think that you've had your weekly intake within the last fifteen minutes."

Matthew said, "That stuff's bollocks, I don't believe in that crap."

"So what about your condition it can't be helping with that surely?"

"Look when I was in hospital. I was prescribed anti-depressants and when I got home, I found Jack Daniels and hookers a much better pick me up than those."

The professor started asking Matthew about his upbringing, his family values, how old he was when he lost his virginity, did he have any pets, what sports he followed, about his marriage, the books he read, the films he watched, the music he listened to, what he did to relax, did he have a hobby, what food he ate, plus many more questions, this continued throughout the flight.

Matthew began to feel pissed off by all these questions. The professor eventually informed Matthew as they were approaching the airport, that while he had enjoyed meeting him, this was no mere meeting of strangers on a flight, only that he had been asked by David Prendergast to carry out a psychological profile of him during the time they spent together on Air Force One.

The professor apologised for being so secretive but explained "I needed to talk to you without you knowing what I was doing."

"Don't worry about it" Matthew said, "I'm beginning to understand the way these people work."

In his head, he thought to himself, *just worry about the kind of profile I will eventually carry out on your daughter,* he started to laugh to himself but could not stop himself laughing out aloud.

The professor said, "Have I said something to amuse you Matthew?"

"No it's just me."

Once the aircraft touched down, the professor's daughter brought them another jug and managed without her father seeing her do it, to palm Matthew a note with her name telephone number and where she was staying in Washington written on it and as luck would have it, she was staying at the Willard hotel. The same place where Gio had told Matthew he would more than likely be staying should he end up in Washington.

After getting off the aircraft Matthew was asked to get into the Presidential limousine along with the President and he was taken directly to the White house, accompanied by four police out riders escorting them right up to the front door.

I could easily get used to this life style, Matthew thought to himself. "Excuse me, sir but will I be staying here during my visit?"

"No I'm sorry Matthew, you won't you'll be staying at the Willard hotel."

Great he thought, *I'm going to enjoy this visit, I'm already on a certainty with Gio's three friends who work at the Willard then the stewardess off the flight and as a last resort there was always Georgia.*

Chapter 8
The Compromise Agreement

The night before the independent hearing, Matthew and Mark met each other for dinner and as they were both staying at the Willard hotel, they chose to eat there as the food had been highly recommended. Matthew remembered something else that was highly recommended and that was Georgia but tonight wasn't the night for that type of thing and anyway he had four other options if he wanted but this visit to Washington was far more important than adding yet another conquest to his ever increasing list. This visit was for business only, as he felt sure that he would be visiting Washington quite a lot in future, so he was going to save the pleasure for some of his other trips.

Matthew and Mark had too much work to do tonight in order to prepare themselves for tomorrow's meeting with President Peterson and besides that he wasn't feeling on top of his game tonight, what with this stupid bandage wrapped around his skull like a Turban.

They both chose their meals from the à la carte menu, both choosing the same main, lobster Thermidor with Dauphinoise potatoes as a side. The waitress came to the table to take their order and Matt being as he was couldn't resist flirting with her, even though tonight was strictly business he still had one eye on the future and he was laying the foundations for his pleasure trips to come.

He asked her "I believe you know Giovanni?"

"Yes I do."

Matthew said "he's a close friend of mine and he told me to look you up if I stayed here and if I mentioned his name you would look after me, I assumed he meant I would get a better room or something like that?"

She replied, "Yes, something like that."

Matthew thought, *good answer*.

However it was vital that tonight they made sure they thought of and prepared for every possible scenario for tomorrow's meeting. Mark was insisting they worked out their strategy for the meeting tomorrow.

"So how do we play this then?" Matthew asked Mark.

"I think that by what you've told me and what I've worked out, there will probably be around ten people there excluding us. So I'm going to make enough copies of the report to take into the meeting and two copies of Sarah's video, one for the hearing and one for the President. Then we explain everything I've been subjected to over the last ten years or so."

"OK but what do we want from it?"

"First of all, an admission from them that they knew of what the medical council did to me and we insist whoever is responsible pay's the price for what they've done by not allowing my treatment to be used and we want an assurance to be able to use it legally from now on."

"OK but what are we prepared to give in return?"

"I think we should give them an assurance, that we will never release any information to the media about what's happened over the last ten years or so."

"OK but what if they won't go for that?"

"Then we release the information as you threatened we would."

"OK they agree and then what?"

"We insist on a press release about miracle."

"What do we say at the press release, about why it hasn't been available for use up to date, even though it was discovered over ten or more years ago?"

"We don't say that. We just say, that we believe we are close to making a major breakthrough with the Miracle cure, however to date we have only carried out tests in the lab on animals."

"What, good will that do?"

"We also inform them, that there is still a lot of work to do before it can be used on humans but we are confident it will be a success but unfortunately it won't be available for use on people for another two years."

"I don't like the sound of that Mark."

"Why not, what's wrong with it?"

"If you think through what you've just said, all we will be doing is condemning hundreds of people to death, who we know could be treated and benefit from the cure today." He then continued, "If we do what you've just proposed, in two year's a lot more people will have died even though we know we have the means to prevent that happening today and more families devastated by the loss of a loved one. So I'm not prepared to go along those lines, just to continue with a cover up to save Peterson and the others responsible for all the murders they have already committed."

"Murders is a bit strong Matthew don't you think?"

"Not in my book it's not and the more I think of this, the more I see it that my wife was murdered by these bastards."

"OK Matthew but let's at least just call it manslaughter shall we?"

"You can call it what you want but the way I see it, they could just as easily taken out a revolver and executed her achieving the same result."

"Matthew you know how much I respect your views but I think it's time you should leave your emotion behind and start thinking a bit more rational."

"Fuck you, with your, emotions and rational thinking, these people are responsible for the death of my wife, plus many hundreds more deaths of people that could and should have been avoided, so don't tell me what to think!"

"OK Matt I'm sorry I shouldn't have said that."

"No you shouldn't Mark."

"Matthew, I think I know what you're going through."

"No you don't, you haven't got a clue because you haven't had to sit there for thirteen weeks waiting and praying for your wife to die, just because she was in a vegetative state with no hope of recovering and knowing that she wouldn't want to spend the rest of her life like that and being relieved when she did eventually die." Matthew was really angry at Mark's comment. "So don't fucking patronise me Mark."

Mark understood that Matthew had a nasty streak in him but was surprised at just how angry he was and for one moment thought Matthew was going to hit him.

"OK Matthew maybe I haven't but I have had to sit there for the last ten years or so, knowing that I had a cure. Yet I let people die because I was too much of a coward to do anything about it and some of those people were friends and even relatives of mine. So I do have some idea of what you have been through."

Matthew could tell from Mark's response, how much he regretted what he had said.

Mark continued, "Plus I realise, how angry and vengeful you are but I'm just trying to be realistic because I know how these bastards work and if we go in too heavy handed we will achieve nothing."

"OK fair point buddy, I know what you mean but it's just the thought of all the suffering over the next two years knowing that we are in a position to help to avoid some of it."

"OK so how about this then? I have enough serum as I've taken to calling it, as it sounds better than dead baby cells." He continued, "I have enough to treat about fifteen hundred people."

Mark's new idea was, "We take this line, we insist that we have a press release, at which we announce the breakthrough we have had with miracle but before it can be used as a general cure for everyone we still have to conduct clinical trials and we are looking for 1500 volunteers to take part in the trials."

Matthew asked "What will that achieve?"

"After the announcement, we pick 1500 who we know are desperate for this treatment and use those, then we will know we will cure at least 1500 people."

"Sounds OK to me that Mark."

"Matthew, even if we released it for general use today, we couldn't treat more than 1500 people any way."

"What if there are more than 1500 Mark?"

"During the trials we will keep harvesting serum and add more people to the list as we go along, so without making an announcement that we will be using the treatment to cure people with immediate effect, that's what we will be doing in actual fact." Mark asked Matthew, "So what do you think about that then?"

"Mark I think you're a genius and even more manipulative than I am and I thought I was good."

"So let's make that our bargaining tool but also be prepared to think on our feet."

"I don't have a problem in that area Mark, I've had to rely on fast thinking all my life, or as some have called it bullshit."

"So what have you got planned for the rest of tonight then Matthew?"

"I just thought I would go up to my room, with a jug and watch a bit of TV and have a smoke on the balcony and get an early night."

"What you're going up by yourself?"

"Yes I am."

"Matt that's the first time I've known you to strike out on your first night in a new city."

"Yes I know but tomorrow's too important, so I will just have to make up for it when this is all over and make no mistake about it make up for it I will."

"What you're already on a promise?"

"Not so much a promise, more of a certainty."

"A certainty; with anyone I know?"

"I don't think so, with a friend of a friend who's called Georgia."

"Goodnight Matthew and get a good night's rest."

"You too Mark, see you down here 8 a.m. for breakfast."

"Yes no problem Matthew."

Mark said to Matthew, "I forgot to tell you earlier, I bet you can't guess who I had dinner with last week?"

"No I can't, so go on and tell me."

"With Ekaterina that's who."

Matthew said, "oh yes, so who's that then?"

"She's your Russian beauty you idiot."

"Hey thanks buddy, that helps for the future and how is she doing?"

"She's fine and she asked me to say hello."

Chapter 9

The Independent Hearing

After a hearty breakfast Mark said, "How is it I feel like the condemned man?"

"Don't worry, just stick to what we agreed last night and we'll be alright and how did you sleep last night Mark?"

"Very well thanks and you?"

"Fine thanks."

When they arrived at the White house they were escorted into the Map Room. Already assembled in there, was the President and a number of people that neither Mathew nor Mark recognised at first. The President announced. "Gentlemen I have called this independent hearing today, due to a claim of mall practice, against both the United Sate's Federal Medical Council and successive U.S. administrations over the past 10 years or more."

He went on to introduce those taking part. "This hearing will examine evidence from Dr Mark Cooper, Mr Matthew Michellin and Professor Andrew Armstrong, the Director General of the Federal Medical Council. The panel will consist of, Washington high court Judge his Honour Graham Lucy and two research scientists, Doctor's Steven Jenkins and Kevin Williams, plus two physicians, Dr Peter

Bartlett and Dr Jonathan Smalling, both general Practitioner's and Monsignor Patrick O'Donnell the head of the Roman Catholic church in the USA."

"The objective of this hearing is to establish the facts behind both of these claims and report the findings back to the Presidential committee for it to decide what action will be taken, if any should be required. If I may now hand over to Washington high court Judge his honour, Graham Lucy, for him to officially open this hearing."

It was now that Mark recognised who he was up against. If he wasn't already nervous, he was now and he felt sick knowing he would be facing Professor Armstrong again.

Judge Lucy began by saying, "Gentlemen and members of the panel, may I remind you that no one is on trial here today, the purpose of this hearing is to establish facts, not innocence or guilt, however the hearing will be carried out under Federal court rules and all evidence will be given under oath and anything discussed during these proceedings will be strictly confidential."

He checked that everyone was happy and that they understood what their roles would be, "before I begin I have to establish if anyone in the room, has met either of our two witnesses before today, or been involved with them in any way or has heard of or been involved in Dr Cooper's treatment?" There was silence in the room, "Seeing that nobody has declared an interest. I will confirm these proceedings are now open."

"Gentlemen I will begin by calling Dr Cooper to the stand. Dr Cooper would you begin by presenting your evidence to the room?"

"Thank you your Honour replied Mark, if I may start with how I first became involved in medicine through to today's proceedings."

"Yes of course Dr Cooper you may begin."

Mark for the second time in recent weeks, went through the whole story from his research team being disbanded and how he had lobbied the Federal Medical Council for funding and how they refused to support him, explaining how Matthew had become involved through to this moment in time. Each one of the people present listened with intent and made notes during Mark's explanation. That is each person present with the exception of Professor Armstrong, in fact to an observer of body language they would probably have described his manner during Mark's explanation as being totally disinterested, however as no one in attendance was an expert his manner generally went unnoticed. That is unnoticed to everyone other than Matthew. It was the Judge who made the first comment. "Dr Cooper I find your testimony absolutely fascinating, yet disturbing as well. Dr Cooper I need to ask you some questions?"

"Of course your Honour how can I help?"

"Dr Cooper I must ask you about the young girl."

"You said you invited her parents to meet you and discuss using your treatment to try to cure her."

"Yes I did," replied Mark.

The Judge continued, "Would you agree that, that could be seen as being a bit irresponsible by the Federal Medical Council?"

"I'm sorry your Honour, I don't understand what you mean?"

"You had no idea whether there would be any the side effects on people, as you have admitted yourself that you hadn't run trials on people."

"That's right your honour, however what I omitted to tell you was that while I hadn't carried out what is accepted as recognised clinical trials on the validity of the cure, I had tested the serum on myself and members of my staff to assess any side effects it may have."

Again Judge Lucy picked Mark up on his answer, saying "and is that not a bit unorthodox Dr Cooper?"

"Yes it is your Honour but due to the restrictions placed upon me I had no other viable option."

"OK Dr Cooper I could see that but my concern is why you would omit such an important piece of information during your testimony?"

"For no particular reason you're Honour, other than I'm just a bit nervous that's all."

"You have no need to be nervous Dr Cooper."

"I'm sorry your Honour, I'm not used to speaking in front of such an esteemed audience."

"Very well, carry on Dr Cooper, just relax were here to try to assist you not to condemn you, however you must realise that it's vital, if we are to understand your evidence you have to tell us everything so we can come to the correct conclusion."

He went on to ask Mark, "Dr Cooper did you get agreement from the young girls parents?"

"Yes I did your Honour."

"Can you tell us the outcome?"

"I think I may be able to do better than that your Honour, as I have video evidence of how she responded to my treatment."

"Very good Dr Cooper, could you show us the evidence?"

Mark played the tape for the team. Everyone watched with amazement and took more notes, once again everyone with the exception of Professor Armstrong.

"Dr Cooper, that is remarkable to say the least but why didn't you present this evidence to the medical council?"

"I did your Honour."

"I'm sorry did you just say you did?"

"That's right your Honour I did."

"You say they still rejected it?"

"I do your Honour."

"I find that incredible, were you given an explanation as to why anyone would reject your treatment following witnessing this evidence?"

"Yes I was."

"What would that be, Dr Cooper?"

"There a number of reasons."

"So could you explain what they were?"

"The first was for financial reasons."

"I'm sorry I don't understand, are you saying it's very expensive to produce?"

"No your Honour I'm not."

"So what are you saying?"

"I'm saying that it was explained to me that a product of this type, would have a disastrous effect on the profitability of the pharmaceutical companies," Mark gave a full explanation.

The Judge said, "I find that unbelievable Dr Cooper, you're saying the medical authorities would reject a medical breakthrough of this magnitude because some companies would lose money!"

"I did as well your honour."

"So Dr Cooper, do you think you could offer a reason why they would say such a thing?"

"I can only speculate on those reasons your Honour but I believe that Professor Armstrong would be better suited to answer that question."

"Tell us why that would be DR Cooper?"

"Your Honour because it was Professor Armstrong who made the comment in the first place that's why."

"I'm sorry Dr Cooper I don't understand what you mean by that."

"You see your Honour it was Professor Armstrong who chaired the meeting that's why."

The whole of the room then let out a groan. Armstrong looked directly at the floor and shifted uneasily in his chair.

"I'm sorry Dr Cooper but I don't understand."

"It's as simple as this your Honour, Professor Armstrong was the Chairman of the committee that banned my treatment from being used."

"Can I ask you to pause for a moment, Dr Cooper?"

"Of course you can."

Judge Lucy continued and said, "Professor Armstrong you were asked to declare any interest in today's proceedings and you failed to do so, can I ask you why?"

Armstrong nervously replied, "I just don't recall ever meeting Dr Cooper before your Honour that's why."

The Judge said to Mark. "Dr Cooper is there any possibility you may have mistaken Professor Armstrong for someone else?"

"No none whatsoever your Honour."

The Judge said, "Gentlemen as it has been such a long and stressful day. I think we should adjourn the meeting for now, is that acccptable to you Mr President?"

"Yes it is Judge Lucy." He continued by saying "Gentlemen I have to apologies for our lack of facilities it would seem we have a problem with the White house kitchens today. I have had to arrange for lunch to be served at the Willard hotel. You will find a fleet of cars outside ready to take you there. Dr Cooper, Mr Michellin and Judge Lucy, could I just have a moment of your time before you leave?" He continued "we will join the rest of you shortly when we've finished."

The President approached Mark and said "Dr Cooper, while, I'm not, doubting what you have said but could there be any way you have mistaken Professor Armstrong for somebody else who may have chaired the meeting?"

"No absolutely none, what so ever, sir."

The President commented, "Very well then, I think Judge Lucy we will have to investigate this claim further."

"I agree sir, I believe we should now conduct a full Judicial enquiry, into today's evidence do you agree sir?"

"Yes I do and how soon could that be arranged?" asked the President.

"I would say within the next fourteen days, as I will have to find an available court room and appoint another Judge to chair the proceedings, as I feel that following today's hearing my impartiality has been compromised somewhat."

"So can I count on you to arrange that?"

"Yes you can sir."

"Thank you, let's go and get something to eat then."

Ten minutes later the four of them entered the dining room where the others were already eating their set meal of roast beef. The Judge announced the need for the judicial enquiry and informed everyone that they would be required to attend. He had already made the arrangements in the car between the Whitehouse and the hotel. It was to be held two weeks today.

Chapter 10
The Judicial Enquiry

Those who were required to attend were assembled in the court room, waiting for the enquiry to begin. The new Judge was sworn in his name was Rudy Melvin, he opened with the normal formalities and told everyone that today's enquiry would be conducted under US Federal law and that those being questioned were to be questioned under oath and that the proceedings would be recorded by a court stenographer. The officials also included two court Bailiffs, the Judge stated that these proceedings were to establish the facts relating to the suppression of miracle and Dr Coopers claim that Professor Armstrong was the Chairman of the panel which originally banned his cure and Professor Armstrong's claim he had been confused for someone else.

The first to be called to the witness stand was Mark, "Please take the bible in your right hand Dr Cooper and take the oath." Dr Cooper, even though you may have already answered some of today's questions at the previous hearing. Owing to me not being present at that hearing, I need you to submit you evidence again." Mark once again relayed his story to the court room. This time professor Armstrong was listening with intent and busy taking notes. The Judge asked the bailiff could you put the tape in to the machine and press play, after viewing the video the Judge said, "That is powerful stuff Dr Cooper. I can understand your annoyance that your treatment was rejected but I don't understand why it was."

"No your Honour neither do I."

"Dr Cooper didn't you claim that it was down to the loss of profit that would be suffered by the pharmaceutical companies?"

Mark replied "that is one of the reasons I was given at the time."

"What were the other ones?"

"Professor Armstrong stated it would reduce the earning potential of the top doctors and scientists."

"Why would that happen? For the time being Dr Cooper could you refrain from naming professor Armstrong and use the term the Chairman? Carry on Dr Cooper."

"The reason is it's the pharmaceutical companies who employ these people to carryout research and if these companies lost money they couldn't afford to fund research projects any longer."

The Judge said, "So it wasn't just concern for the companies but their own greed as well?"

"Yes I believe that it was your Honour."

"Was there anything else?"

"It was also claimed, that if we found a cure for all ailments, what would be the point of future research, as we already have a miracle cure-all."

"God forbid that ever happening Dr Cooper, as life just wouldn't be worth living if we didn't have an illness that would eventually kill us."

Everyone with the exception of professor Armstrong gave a little chuckle at the Judge's comment.

"All joking aside Dr Cooper, what an absolutely ridiculous statement to make as a reason for not developing your treatment."

"There was also NASA."

"Sorry, that one needs an explanation."

"It was claimed that as the pharmaceuticals financed all recent trips to the international space station to conduct research in a different type of atmosphere and the assess the negative effect low gravity has on the human body and that no profit means no more space trips."

"Any further reasons, Dr Cooper?"

"Yes there was your Honour."

"So what were they?"

"It was claimed that the Government would lose votes because of this treatment."

"Why would that be?"

"I have to apologise for this Father, these are not my words I'm just paraphrasing what I was told."

"Go on Dr Cooper."

"It was claimed, the Bible basher's and religious nuts would be up in arms at my cure and that the Government would lose all their votes."

"Dr Cooper, I'm lost by what you have just said, so you will have to explain?"

"Your Honour it was claimed my treatment was tantamount to playing God and interfered with nature and life."

The Judge replied, "But couldn't that be said of every time we administer a drug that saves a life?"

"Yes it could."

"Also another thing Dr Cooper, I'm under the impression that stem cell treatment is something that is carried out almost daily in the US already."

"That's right your Honour it is."

"So why is your treatment such a problem?"

"It's like this your Honour, the difference with stem cell treatment being administered today and mine, is that current treatment utilises Adult stem cells harvested from a live donor, whereas mine are harvested from a dead foetus and that's where the controversy lies and is viewed by numerous people of being unethical."

"So why can't the same results be achieved by stem cell treatment that's currently in use?"

"The main reason is your Honour, Adult stem cells risk rejection by the recipient due to the stem cells already having the donor's own cellular fingerprint or identity and are treated just like any other foreign body entering our body and our immune system produces antibodies and fights them."

"Can't we do something about this rejection?"

"Yes we can prescribe drugs to fight his rejection but those drugs reduce the effectiveness of our own immune system, leaving the recipient susceptible to further serious illnesses."

"So why are yours so successful?"

"Your Honour, infant stem cells taken from a foetus have no prior identity, or previous cellular fingerprint known as antigenicity and as such are unique and are able to assume the identity of the recipient and become part of our own unique bodies building blocks waiting to be pieced together as they search for the damaged area of the body and repair or replace the damaged cells and they also supplement and strengthen our own immune system."

"Sound's fascinating DR Cooper but a bit like science fiction to me, could you explain for all our understanding the full reason why foetal stem cells are so controversial?"

"Yes I can because there isn't a way to guarantee we have enough available cells other than through abortion and there is a fear that people will be encouraged or rewarded to have an abortion to make the cells available."

"Could there be any truth in that Dr Cooper?"

"No none at all your Honour, in fact it would be less likely."

"Why's that Dr Cooper?"

"Regardless of how much we campaign against them, abortions will always take place your Honour, even if they become back street again. So by making my treatment a part of our fight against serious illness we can guard against this, as we can regulate the use and the harvesting of the cells."

"How could you do that Dr Cooper?"

"Simply by legislation, education and ensuring we only harvest cells from recognised and authorised sources, meaning we only use cells from donors who have been screened and had all the medical checks prior to the abortion taking place and we only accept cells from donors who have had an abortion due to a medical or psychological condition that could affect the mother and that the donor gives permission for the cells to be used in the way we want them to be and that any abortion from which we can receive harvested cells, come from hospitals that are on a specific register and are harvested by licenced medical teams and it can be confirmed the abortion has taken place for the correct reasons and the donor doesn't benefit financially and also by educating the general public to the criminality of what happens to an aborted foetus."

"Can you explain what you mean by that please?"

"Yes I can, you see your Honour once a foetus has been aborted It's treated as clinical waste in the same way as used bandages, dressings, syringes, amputated limbs, or removed organs and contaminated blood, etc."

"Treated in what way, Dr Cooper?"

"Your Honour at the end of each day, it's bagged and thrown into an incinerator, along with all the other waste and that's where the true crime lies, you see from each foetus we can harvest enough of the cells to treat and save the lives of hundreds of patients."

"OK I think I'm beginning to understand now, Dr Cooper."

"That's why it so criminal, we have a resource here that is just being wasted. Simply because of so called ethics."

"Dr Cooper, could you provide us with a layman's understanding of how it works as part of your evidence?"

"Your Honour we are still unsure why they do what they do but we do know that they do it."

"That doesn't help my understanding Dr Cooper, not one bit."

"If I may, use Matthew to demonstrate your Honour?"

"Of course if he is willing."

"No problem your Honour," Matthew agreed.

Mark asked Matthew to stand up and began to explain why Matthew was as he was. "You see your Honour, Matthew seems perfectly normal yet his condition is a result of a brain infraction, otherwise known as a stroke and during his stroke, damage was caused to cells and neurons in his brain and it's these neurons that enable us all to carry out our cognitive functions and once these cells have been damaged they are destroyed and sufferers, while their intellect may not be impaired, their mobility is and with the use of foetal stem cells, my treatment can reverse this damage, allowing the recipient to live a fully active life once again. To date we don't have a conventional treatment to repair this damage therefore leaving the patient with a permanent disability. We have discovered that by using foetal stem cells we can repair and reverse the condition to enable the brain to function as it did prior to the damage taking place. If you think of a building your Honour that is in need of repair, we employ a tradesman to bring along the necessary materials to repair it and stem cells are those materials and I am one of the tradesmen,"

"Remarkable Dr Cooper but you don't know why it does this."

"No not really but we do know how, you see the cells as I've explained find their way to the damaged part of the body and assume the identity of that damaged part and then become a clone. But why it does this we don't know but we know it does."

"You originally said it repaired the damage to the brain, then you said body was that just a slip of the tongue?"

"No your Honour it wasn't."

"So are you saying your treatment doesn't only repair brain damage?"

"Yes I am."

"So what do you mean by that?"

"I mean they will repair cells in other parts of the body as well."

"Do you mean cancerous cells?"

"Yes but not on their own your Honour, however they will enable our bodies to cope with much higher doses of current treatment therefore attacking the tumour in a more aggressive way but this side of my research is really only in It's infancy, however I do have a considerable amount of confidence that it will also revolutionise the treatment of this condition. They will also help in the treatment of damaged organs, which could lead to the demand for organ donation being a thing of the past."

"Thank you, Dr Cooper."

"You're welcome, but could I just add something your Honour, this is most definitely science fact and not science fiction."

"Thank you again Dr Cooper but I do have one more question and that is what can't they do?"

"Well your Honour they can't reverse the aging process. Although they can increase your vitality."

"Did you just say vitality or virility?"

"I said vitality but after trailing it on my staff, some did claim their virility had increased and I also experienced that as well."

Matthew's ear's pricked up like a startled rabbit when he heard this and the Judge said, "I need to keep that information from my wife."

"They can't re-generate a limb or an organ."

"Hang on didn't you just make the claim that due to your treatment, organ donation could become a thing of the past?"

"Yes I did but not as a result of organ re-generation but by helping the damaged organ recover and function as well as it should."

"Will there ever be a chance that one day they can?"

"All I can say to that your Honour is I don't know but the more we use them the more we will understand about them."

"Thank you Dr Cooper you may now stand down. I now call Professor Armstrong to the stand and to take, the oath."

The Judges first question was Professor Armstrong, what we have just heard from Dr Cooper, could I ask you for your opinion of what he explained to us about his treatment?"

"I have to say your Honour, that I find it rather fanciful to say the least!"

"Is that so Professor?"

"Yes it is, he even admits himself he has no idea of how it works, so how can he predict its success?"

"Well Professor Armstrong, wouldn't it be fair to say that throughout the journey of our medical knowledge, we haven't always understood why cures have worked even though we know they have and the most recent example I can bring to mind, would be that while some doctors would wash their hands prior to treating a patient they didn't know it was the most effective way of preventing cross contamination and that it's only in the middle of the last century, that a little known Hungarian lab technician discovered the reason for this?"

"Well yes your Honour but that's hardly the same as claiming you have discovered a miracle cure and not knowing why?"

"Professor Armstrong you have witnessed the video evidence and while Dr Cooper may not be able explain the science behind it, it's obviously cured the youngster you cannot deny it's worked."

"I'm sorry your Honour but that's the problem, has it worked, or is there another explanation for the girl's recovery?"

"Do you mean you are agreeing with the original reason why the committee rejected it as one of those so called acts of God?"

"I have to say, that to me it's as plausible as Dr Cooper's theory. I would need a lot more proof of other patients who have recovered, due to Dr Cooper's claims."

"Isn't that why we are here today professor is it not. If the medical council had accepted his treatment we would already have that proof. So I don't accept that just because we don't know exactly how it works that we shouldn't use it."

The Judge continued. "As long as we know that patients suddenly don't acquire a third eye which I think would be unlikely."

"That for me, your Honour, is the biggest reason not to use the treatment. If we don't know why it does what it does, how can we possibly predict what it won't do and in my opinion it would be irresponsible to give it to patients today not knowing what it could turn into in future generations."

"Professor Armstrong talking of fanciful, that's exactly how I find your statement and at the moment I would describe it as nothing more than scaremongering."

Judge Melvin continued, "I'm sure your next comment will have us believing that because of Dr Cooper mankind will eventually turn into nothing more than, a world of mutants."

"I wouldn't go quite that far but I think it is a better reason for not using it, than NASA not being able to fly to Mars."

"OK professor I have a few more relevant questions that I would like you to answer. Do you have any financial involvement with any of the pharmaceutical companies?"

"I'm sorry your Honour but in what way do you mean?"

"Let me make it simple for you to understand. Do you receive payments from any of these companies, for any work you do on their behalf?"

"In that way do you mean, your Honour?"

"Professor I'm sure you should be able to understand that question."

"Yes I do help them with research."

"Is that all, professor?"

"No I also endorse some of their products."

"Is that all now professor?"

"No I also attend some of their seminars as a guest speaker."

"Hang on professor, I understand that you are trying to avoid answering my first question but however many question's it takes I will get the answer. So to save everyone's time, why don't you just tell us all exactly what involvement you have with these companies?"

"Your Honour along with the ones I've already mentioned. I am also on the board of two of these companies as well."

"So that would mean you would lose a considerable amount of your income if these companies cease trading."

"Yes I suppose I would, but so would a lot of other Doctors and Scientists."

"Professor Armstrong I'm not interested in other Doctors or Scientists, so could you tell the court just how much money you would lose?"

"I'm sorry you Honour I can't recall how much that would be."

"Well can I ask you what you earned last year?"

"I'm sorry your Honour I don t know without speaking to my accountant."

"Could you hazard a guess, as to how much as a percentage of your income these companies contributed to your overall salary last year?"

"I couldn't say your Honour as I don't recall, I would need to get that information from my accountant."

"Professor Armstrong, Dr Cooper claimed you were the Chairman of the committee that he presented his evidence to and you said you weren't. Is that still your claim?"

"Yes it is your Honour, I can't recall ever meeting Dr Cooper before our meeting in the White house."

"Thank you professor, I have no further questions but before you stand down does anyone else have any questions?"

Mark said "I do your Honour, professor Armstrong you have just claimed that we had not met prior to meeting in the White house."

"That's right we haven't."

"Could I remind you that just over four years ago I applied for a post as a neurological consultant, at the psychiatric hospital, at Kimball New Jersey and that you were on the interview, panel."

"I'm sorry Dr Cooper, I do not recall that occasion, as I have sat on many interview panels in the last four years and I can't possibly be expected to remember every person, who didn't get the job."

Armstrong continued "may I make a point your Honour?"

"Of course professor Armstrong if you think it could help."

"Thank you your Honour," he then turned to Mark and said "even though I don't recall the interview taking place,

Dr Cooper, I have to say, if you have confused me with someone else, could it be because that person rejected you. You're holding a grudge against whomever you've confused me with and this is your reason for making these bogus claims?"

Everyone with the exception of Mark and Matthew thought that Armstrong had a valid point, his first so far!

"Thank you professor Armstrong you may now stand down."

"Could I now call Mr Michellin to the stand?"

Matthew went through the formalities and the first question was.

"Mr Michellin could I ask you what is your motivation for becoming involved in this fight alongside Dr Cooper, we can all understand Dr Coopers motivation but I have confess that I'm still struggling to understand yours?"

Matthew looked confused by the question and the Judge continued, "So can I suggest that you're no more than an opportunist, who saw an easy way of making money because it was you was it not, who made the threats to release this information, no doubt hoping to sell your story to the highest bidder, or we're you thinking of blackmailing the Government or the individuals you assumed were involved in this so called suppression and make yourself a very wealthy man?"

"Well your Honour that's quite a lot of questions for me to answer, so if I can I will try to answer them all at once if I may?"

"Go ahead, Mr Michellin."

"What a load of shite that is!"

"I beg your pardon, Mr Michellin!"

"I'm sorry your Honour that's an English phrase, I should have put it in terms you could understand, I meant to say what a load of crap that is."

"Again, Mr Michellin, I beg your pardon, I wasn't asking you to translate I was making a statement about how rude your outburst was."

"I'm sorry your Honour I will try to answer your questions in the way I think everyone can understand, what you said about me was the biggest load of fucking bullocks I've ever heard in all my life."

Mark almost wet himself while trying to hold in the laughter that was bursting his lungs to escape but he thought to himself *Oh no, Matt, don't be a jerk.*

The Judge's face was almost purple with rage and he said, "Mr Michellin, any more outburst's like that and I will hold you in contempt of court."

"OK your Honour, none of them are the reasons why I am involved in this other than I do hope to have some personal gain and that is I hope to benefit from Dr Cooper's cure, that amongst other reasons, but my personal gain has nothing to do with seeing my bank account growing, money has never even entered my head during my involvement in this."

He continued, "You have just witnessed my disability and all you've seen is the cosmetics of my condition, you have no idea how my life has been affected by this condition, not only is this a physical disability, it's also affected my emotional state of mind, my confidence my personality, my independence, so yes I do hope to gain from my involvement with Dr Cooper and that is to be administer his treatment and recover from my illness, you see I was always in control and set the rules, whereas now I have no control and I have to follow everybody else's rules, I used to be a very young middle aged man, now I'm nothing more than a very old middle aged man, who has to rely on the kindness of my family and friends to get through life, I don't know if you can understand how frustrating that can be but not only that your Honour. I have also suffered through the loss of a loved one, who could still be alive today if Dr Cooper had been allowed to use his treatment on her and for me that is a bigger motivation than even my own recovery."

"So why exactly is that Mr Michellin?"

"Your Honour is that a serious question? I know what it's like to lose your wife and how her death, has affected me and so many people, most of who still haven't and I suppose never will get over her death. You see she died as a result of a stroke, during the time this cure should have been available to treat her."

"Also my motivation is, I don't see why families have to go through this grief when there is no need too and my intention was and still is, is to get this treatment used to save lives and stop any further unnecessary grief. Plus making sure those responsible for the suppression of this miracle cure pay the price for all the unnecessary deaths and suffering they've caused."

"Is that so and what price do you suggest that should be Mr Michellin?"

"Your Honour, I see this as a crime against humanity and if some despot somewhere was responsible for the countless number of lives' lost through their tyranny, as have been lost due to banning Mark's treatment, the world would deem that a war crime and call for appropriate action taken to bring them to justice, your Honour and I see these people in the same light. So I do want these people punished. You see I see this comparable to mass murder, so in my mind I think they should face the death penalty!"

"If any charges are brought against anyone Mr Michellin I can't see it being anything more than manslaughter."

"OK so jail them for life then but don't let them walk away from this despicable act and that your Honour is my motivation and another thing, I was informed by Mark right from the start, that my involvement in this could result in my life being under threat, due to the embarrassment caused to the authorities, who would try to stop me exposing this to the world."

"Very well Mr Michellin how did you find out about Dr Cooper?"

"Your Honour I was on holiday with a friend of mine when I met him."

He told the Judge the whole story.

"So let me try to understand all of this. You say, you first met Dr Cooper in a bar and spent the whole day and that evening drinking together?"

"Yes we did."

"You say the following day as well and you have met each other on several occasions since?"

"Yes we have."

"Have those occasion's also included copious amounts of alcohol as well?"

"I wouldn't say copious amounts but some alcohol yes they have."

"It's on these occasions that you say you can recall with absolute clarity everything Dr Cooper has told you, including your life being in danger?"

"Yes that's right your Honour it is."

"Mr Michellin, I have a physiological profile, about your personality which was put together by a Harvard professor recently during a flight you took together and I notice how much alcohol you consumed even before the aircraft left the ground. It also mentions your obsession with the opposite sex, suggesting you have very low self-esteem and that all this womanising and drinking, is just a very insecure person trying to seek attention and acceptance back into normal society to compensate for your insecurity and also that your involvement in this affair is just a means of making you feel important once again and a way of seeking attention and validation. He concluded that you're suffering with a condition known as N.P.D. otherwise Known as Narcissistic Personality Disorder. How would you respond to that Mr Michellin?"

Even before Matthew had time to consider his answer Mark thought, *oh no why did you ask him to comment your Honour?*

Matthew responded by saying.

"You really do come out with some shit over here, what a load of fucking bollocks that is. Your psychopath is nothing more than a fucking prick and a quack."

"Mr Michellin I have already warned you about your behaviour, may I remind you, that you are in a US court of law and outbursts of that nature will not be tolerated and Mr Michellin he is a psychologist not a psychopath."

"They both begin with psycho don't they, so no fucking difference they both mean the fucking same to me, sorry your Honour about my language it was just a figure of speech."

"Could you please refrain from using figures of speech of that kind so we can all understand your testimony?"

"Sorry your honour but I don't understand this character assassination by you on me."

"It's not a character assassination, I'm just trying to understand your personality and your credibility as a reliable witness and I have to say Mr Michellin from the personality profile I have of you and my own opinion of you today it confirms what I expected to see."

"So what was that, your Honour?"

"That was and is, that you're nothing other than an unreliable, vengeful, storytelling, alcoholic who is clearly in need of counselling and therapy."

Matthew again morphed into the green eyed monster that has got him into so much trouble throughout his life and this time there was no holding back.

"Are you sure you're fucking qualified enough to chair this hearing because that is just another load of fucking shite, fuck you and fuck your counselling."

The Judge could hardly get his breath.

"Bailiff, could you escort Mr Michellin to the bench please. Mr Michellin I've already warned you about your behaviour."

"Sorry again your Honour, just another figure of speech."

"Sorry isn't good enough this time Mr Michellin and that figure of speech has just cost you a thousand Dollars and any more figures of speech of that nature will see you spending a night or two in somewhere other than the Willard hotel and by the way I will have you know my Alma Mater was Harvard law school, so what do you think about that Mr Michellin?"

"I haven't a clue because I don't what it means."

"Alma Mater means your place of education, you can now stand down now Mr Michellin."

Matthew immediately sat next to Mark and said to him "What a fucking idiot he Is."

Mark replied "figure of speech Matthew, figure of speech."

"Bollocks asshole" replied Matthew.

The Judge adjourned the enquiry until 9 a.m. the next morning.

Chapter 11
The Conclusion

When the enquiry reconvened the following morning the Judge announced, he had come to a decision after consultation with the President.

"I think we will start with Mr Michellin." The Judge continued, "In Mr Michellin we believe, we have a witness who has no financial motivation due to his involvement with Dr Cooper but we do advise him to seek professional help with his alcohol problems and find a top Psychologist to help him cope with his personality disorders." The Judge continued "I'm pleased to say that the President will be personally involved to find and also finance the best possible help for Mr Michellin."

He continued by saying. "As we both believe a vengeful alcoholic is a very dangerous person and Mr Michellin your continued involvement with the miracle project depends on your cooperation and you seeking help with these issues that seem to have consumed your life."

Mark put his hand over his ear's expecting to hear a tirade of abuse from Matthew and thought to himself, *I think I will be dining by myself tonight,* but breathed a sigh of relief when all he heard Matthew say was.

"Thank you, your Honour."

The Judge himself seemed almost relieved and surprised by Matthews's response.

"Next I think we should talk about Dr Cooper. Both the President and I have agreed that what Dr Cooper has achieved through his research and his tenacity he deserves recognition for his achievement and not obstruction by the authorities. The President has stated. He will now be provided with any funds and facilities within the US that he requires to continue with his work. It was also agreed that the treatment should be kept evolving and that the trials should be carried out with immediate effect and the list should be compiled using the criteria he has suggested and that under no circumstance should favouritism or connection be used as a reason for anybody to be placed on the list."

He continued, "We feel that the concerns of the general public and the church should be paramount and once we are ready to announce the details behind Miracle. We should launch a campaign to ensure everyone knows how ethical this treatment is. The President is going to ensure that it is written into law that all medical checks must be carried out before an aborted foetus can be used to harvest the stem cells and with immediate effect we will advise all hospitals of the need to harvest stem cells from an aborted foetus and we should all be grateful for Dr Cooper's work on this treatment. I personally would like to add that I see this treatment as the greatest medical discovery since penicillin." He turned to Armstrong and said.

"Now can we address the issue with professor Armstrong? Who we believe is an unreliable witness, as he has claimed continually he has never met Dr Cooper before, well one of the advantages of my role is that I can request any information from anywhere, to help with the decision making process and some of the information I requested and received are the records of who he has interviewed for any position in the medical profession over the last ten years and Professor Armstrong I have clear evidence that you did interview Dr Cooper for the position he spoke of yesterday and that it was you who insisted, he not be offered the post, you also conducted an investigation into his background to try to find something you could use against him and I even have you own signed recommendation, that says you believe Dr Cooper to be very dangerous man owing to his opinions on how brain disorders are treated and how he goes against all accepted conventional methods and that we should try to find a way as soon as we can to discredit him and have him removed from the medical register, professor Armstrong I'm sure with this personal vendetta against Dr Cooper, it would be highly unlikely you would ever forget meeting him, so why would you deny ever meeting Dr Cooper when this evidence clearly proves you have?"

"As I said yesterday your Honour, I can't be expected to remember every person I have ever interviewed."

"Professor Armstrong you seem to have a very convenient memory loss. I asked you yesterday about your salary and what proportion of your salary, was paid to you by the pharmaceutical companies and you conveniently couldn't recall those details either. Professor Armstrong as I mentioned before I have access to almost every record, I need to help me form a conclusion to the relevance of somebodies evidence and I'm sure you won't be surprised to learn professor Armstrong that I can remind you of the details your accountant submitted to the I.R.S. on your behalf last year and they confirm that you claimed your salary was a staggering 3.4 million dollars of which 2.2 million was Paid to you by the pharmaceutical companies. Which suggests you did have a very strong financial reason for Dr Cooper's treatment being suppressed, would you agree professor?"

"I would if I had been aware of my payments from these companies."

"I'm sorry professor but did you submit these details to your accountant?"

"Yes I did."

"So I suggest you knew very well how much money you earned last year when I asked you yesterday, so why didn't you, give an honest answer?"

"I did give an honest answer I said I couldn't recall it and I couldn't."

The Judge replied, "Just like you couldn't recall meeting Dr Cooper, even though you have been trying to wreak his career ever since!"

"That's right your Honour I don't recall ever meeting him before."

"So professor, this evidence suggest your lack of recollection to being Chairman the committee, as Dr Cooper claims you were, is just another convenient loss of memory."

"My judgement regarding your testimony is that it is nothing more than a pack of lies and you do in fact recall being responsible for the decision to suppress this treatment, or are you still going to deny that professor?"

"As I have previously said, if I was on the committee I just can't recall it."

"Is that you final answer professor?"

"It is your Honour I just can't recall that meeting ever taking place."

"Professor Armstrong, I have been informed of some facts not discussed at yesterday's proceedings but due to the relevance and the importance of these facts. I am going to allow them to be used as submersible evidence today. You see professor, Dr Cooper is very meticulous in his record keeping and prior to yesterday's hearing, Dr Cooper submitted to the President a list of your co members of the council and everyone on the list with the exception of you have admitted they were part of the decision to reject Dr Cooper's treatment and they have also confirmed the threats to his career were made if he continued with his claim about his treatment and each one confirmed you were the Chairman of the committee, so what do you have to say for yourself about that claim?"

"Your Honour I don't think it's fair that these allegations were not put to me yesterday, so I could answer and give my reply to them."

"I'm sure if they had professor, that your answer would have been I just don't recall those details your Honour."

"That is pure speculation, your Honour."

"So are you saying your co-members are lying?"

"How can I answer that, if I don't even know who these people are, as you haven't told me their names?"

"Professor Armstrong all of your co-conspirators have been taken into custardy and will eventually be charged with conspiracy to defraud the Federal Medical Authorities and gross dereliction of duty. So professor I'm sure it won't be long before you will be meeting the other members on the list and I'm sure once you do you will be able to get your memory refreshed by them."

The Judge called over the bailiff and passed him a note and asked him to pass this note to the President informing him that the enquiry had been concluded and that they would be arriving at the Whitehouse within the hour to discuss the recommendations of the enquiry team with him and could he provide transport for all the attendees.

He then said "Gentlemen I thank you all for your time and involvement into these proceedings and I would now like to announce the enquiry is closed, however as we have all spent a great deal of time on this issue, I would like to conclude everything today and deliver my findings and recommendations but first I have to discuss these with the President, so if we can take an hour's recess and meet back here in one hour, we will then be transported to the Whitehouse where I will announce the recommendations of the enquiry team, thank you gentlemen and I will see you all back here in one hour's time."

Following the hour, they were all transported to the Whitehouse and taken straight into the Map room. The Judge and the other members of the panel were then taken into a separate room to discuss the details with Peterson. The rest of the group sat patiently waiting for the others to come back into the map room, nobody was saying a word.

The President and the others entered the map room with two secret service agents accompanying them; they all sat across the table facing the witnesses. The President welcomed them all and announced that Judge Rudy Melvin will now inform them of the findings and recommendations.

The Judge started by saying, "We have come to our decision and that is. I have already said that Dr Cooper should be rewarded for his work and be given every assistance in perfecting this treatment and receive full recognition for his discovery and Mr Michellin should be encouraged to seek counselling."

He continued, "We now have to deal with professor Armstrong and we all agree that his testimony could not be relied on and we believe he does have a case to answer, owing to his despicable treatment of Dr Cooper and that a person carrying so much responsibility should have at least referred Dr Cooper's findings onto other medical experts to ascertain its value to society, but his reason for not doing so was driven by his financial greed, so we recommend he is charged, along with the other committee members, with conspiracy to defraud the Federal medical Authority and with gross neglect of his responsibility and that he should be removed from his position as Director General, of the Federal Medical Council."

Armstrong's reaction at hearing he was to lose his job was unexpected, as all he did was shrug his shoulders and unbelievably he gave a wry smile as if he didn't care, in truth he was thinking *well I've got off lightly it could have been a lot worse, I was expecting more than just that and based on what was said before I even expected to go to straight jail.*

It was as if Judge Melvin could read his mind, so not to disappoint him he said to Armstrong. "Professor you seem quite satisfied with your punishment but maybe that smile on your face won't be as obvious when I've finished telling you the full extent of it. In addition to being removed from your position of Director General of the Federal Medical council you are to be struck off for life as a practicing doctor with immediate effect and you will also relinquish your pension rights."

"We have also taken into account Mr Michellin's claims that the people responsible for suppressing this treatment should face criminal charges but that will be a decision taken by a Grand jury, we are recommending it should be considered those involved in this despicable decision face multiple manslaughter charges."

"Bailiff would you take Professor Armstrong into custody please and contact the police department to collect him from here?" Armstrong had most definitely lost the smirk on his face, and his legs almost buckled following the Judge's statement, the person smiling most in the room was Mark. The Judge continued, "Gentlemen I find it difficult to claim that this enquiry has been a success, as I feel that this has been a tragic period in US medical history and we would like to apologise to Mr Michellin for his pain and suffering during the past ten years, due to this gross dereliction of responsibility by these committee members, in particular professor Armstrong and also to thank Dr Cooper and to inform you all, that Dr Cooper is to be recommended to the Nobel committee, to be considered for the Noble prize for medicine."

Everyone other than Armstrong broke into spontaneous applause and started to congratulate Mark.

The Judge continued, "I would like to announce that Dr Cooper's treatment will be used with immediate effect and that at the earliest time we will hold a press release about this remarkable cure. However none of these proceedings or their findings will be made public knowledge."

The President said, "Thank you gentlemen and I feel I must echo the Judge's instruction that these proceedings and conclusions are to be kept completely secret."

Matthew and Mark went straight back to the Willard hotel, if anyone had seen them as they left the White house they would have thought they had just won the lottery, as they both had the biggest smiles on their faces you could have ever seen. On entering the hotel they both went straight into the bar they sat down at a table in the corner and gave each other a triumphal high five.

Matthew said "I think a drink is in order."

Mark said. "Hang on there you drunken bum, do you think that's wise knowing the problems you have."

"Piss off you prick," was Matthew's reply.

He called over his favourite waitress and ordered a jug of Manhattan and a bottle of Dom Perignon.

Matthew said to Mark.

"Time for celebration I think and now business is over, it's also time for pleasure."

He immediately started to work his charm on the waitress and insisted she joined them for a celebration drink but Matt being Matt didn't stop there, he invited her to dinner that evening and while he was waiting for a reply, he had Georgia on his mind.

He received the answer he wanted and arranged to meet at 9.30 p.m. in the bar. Georgia will just have to wait once again. Even though the day had been a success Matthew seemed a bit subdued.

Mark asked him why he looked so solemn, as they had achieved what they had set out to do.

"You look almost disappointed Matthew," was Mark's comment.

Matthew replied, "I don't want to sound ungrateful but I'm now thinking that if these bastards had accepted this treatment when you first presented it. I wouldn't have lost the last six years of my life and my wife would most probably still be alive, so while I'm delighted we've won I'm sad for all the people who have suffered for no reason and those we have lost who can't be returned to us."

"Matthew This Judgement will be of most benefit to new sufferers and people like yourself, who are still suffering."

"Yes I know but how many people have lost their lives because of these murdering bastards and how does this judgement help them."

"At least the truth will soon be out, Matthew."

"Yes the truth that we have a treatment that uses foetal stem cells but will the whole truth ever be known about why for so long have the medical authorities kept this a secret?"

"I don't know, Matthew, but what good will that do anyway, if it does come out, it seems to me that what you're looking for now is retribution."

"That's right I am and why shouldn't I?"

"Matthew until I met you I never thought I would ever be at this stage, so I'm just going to live in the moment for now and then decide what to do if the whole truth should ever come out."

"OK, Mark, I have to go now, I've got some urgent business to attend to."

"So what's that, Matthew?"

"Just to return the compliment to a particular Psychologist and conduct my own psychological profile on a member of his family, that's all."

"I don't really know, what you mean by that but knowing you I would bet it's got something to do with taking your clothes off."

"You're beginning to know me to well, Mark."

"Matthew other than the fact you want to sleep with every woman on earth and have already managed most of them. I don't know anything about you at all, who you are, what are your likes and dislikes?"

"Not another psychological profile buddy?"

"No just a friend wanting to understand what makes you tick.

"I do like the company of the opposite sex."

"Your joking I would never have guessed, come on what sounds do you like, the things you like, that type of thing?"

"Believe it or not but I'm a romantic at heart, I like to romance women and I like being in love, I like the sound of rain, the sound of a dog drinking water from its bowl, thunder, I like to laugh and I even like to cry sometimes, I also like to make people laugh, I like cold crisp sunny mornings, the beach, the sun, honesty, the fall, Christmas, a babies laugh, Jazz, swing, most music, family, socialising, travel but most of all I like waking up in the morning next to someone I'm in love with." Matthew couldn't keep this up much longer and said to Mark, "This is like a dating profile, are you going to ask me to sleep with you later Mark?"

"You know for a couple of minutes Matthew I thought you were normal but then you proved what a philistine you really are."

Chapter 12
The Press Release

It was decided that the press release was to be a glitzy affair put together by a top US media marketing company. The whole presentation was in recognition of progress throughout the whole of the 20th century and this part of the 21st century and it was staged as well as any Hollywood film premier would be. The room was illuminated by lasers which created the word Miracle on each of the walls, the ceiling and the floor and was constantly circling the room. There had been a stage erected so the presenter's would be above the TV cameras and the members of the press and on the wall behind those making the announcement was a gigantic digital TV screen which had the word Miracle continually flashing on and off.

In the centre of the stage was President Peterson and standing directly beside him was the UK PM directly behind them being shown on the giant screen was images and newsreels of significant events and discoveries throughout the 20th and this part of 21st century, beginning with transportation and how the horse drawn carriage had developed into the motorcar and a still image of Henry Ford, then moving onto flight, beginning with the Wright brothers first manned flight at Kitty hawk and through the different stages of manned flight finally ending with a newsreel of Air Force One in flight. Then a section about sea travel. Followed by a short coverage of space exploration beginning with a newsreel of JFK's famous speech about America's intention of landing a man on the moon by the end of the 1960s and a still image of Neil Armstrong stepping down from the Eagle onto the surface of the moon and the word's One small step for man superimposed on the image, continuing through to today's space shuttle and the space lab. It was all very much geared to American triumphalism. Followed by a short section on the industrial revolution highlighting Britain's and in particular Manchester's contribution in this field and continuing, inappropriately as some of the audience thought with a section on war fare and weapon's development throughout the same period, inappropriately, as the world seemed to be on the brink of WW3 owing to Peterson's treatment of and threats to North Korea.

So far nobody had said a word and the audience was becoming restless and confused as to what all this was about. The video continued with a section on medicine and medical breakthrough finally concluding with an attempt, to forecast what may happen in the rest of this and the next century and at the end of show projected onto the screen was a still image of Mark, with the words today's guest speaker and his name flashing on and off and constantly changing colour and when the TV screen was turned off and The President started to speak, the audience broke into spontaneous applause, the lights and lasers were dimmed leaving just a spot light illuminating the microphones, the video section of the press release had already lasted for over 30 minutes, once the video ended it was hard to fathom out whether the cheers were for the President or the fact the film was over but once the President started to speak, everyone in the room was completely focused on what he had to say. He began with a brief explanation, for the reason behind today's gathering and the previous 30 minutes.

"Ladies and Gentlemen we have just witnessed some remarkable innovations throughout the previous 100 years, or so and at the time they were announced, some people couldn't believe what they was being told and were very sceptical, about many of today's day to day thing's we now take for granted."

He continued by saying.

"The same I'm sure will be said about tonight's announcement. Which I believe will eclipse most of what you have just witnessed in our review of previous discoveries."

"Could I ask you all to save any question about our announcement until our presentation has been concluded? It gives me great pleasure to introduce our guest speaker. Dr Mark Cooper."

Mark took the microphone, "Thank you Mr President."

He started his presentation by saying. "I would like to thank all of tonight's members of the press and TV audiences worldwide for their attendance. I will get straight to the point of this TV and press announcement."

"Ladies and Gentlemen you have just witnessed mankind's remarkable technological progress throughout the last 100 years or so, unfortunately we didn't have time to show all the significant inventions and discoveries during our video review, we could have easily spent the next five hours just highlighting how the microchip had changed our lives and we didn't touch on social and economic changes. Such as how civil rights have become a fundamental part of our lives, in particular in the Southern U.S. States and in South Africa and how our lives have changed as a result and how equality is now taken for granted in most areas of our world because of the bravery of people like Dr King and the Reverend Nelson Mandela, who helped bring about these changes. We recognise that we still have a considerable amount of work to do, however we do seem to be winning the fight against poverty and hunger even on the African continent, due to the co-operation of countless countries with the development new crop technology and I'm sure it won't be long before we win the battle against religious intolerance, however we still have one major challenge to overcome and that's the fight against cancer and other life-threatening illnesses plus disability."

The audience were becoming even more restless.

"It is with this in mind we have called you all together tonight, to inform you of our progress in this area and while we still have a considerable way to go to before we can say we have won this war. We can announce that we are winning a fair few battles against these unrelenting enemies, if we could equate this fight in terms of a war, it would be fair to say we have negotiated a cease fire and are well on the way to getting our enemies to surrender and sign a peace treaty."

Mark decided it was time to mention Matthew.

"My good friend and colleague Mr Matthew Michellin and I, have been doing a considerable amount of work, trying to win this war."

The first question came from the floor it was from the member of the BBC.

"Dr Cooper may I ask a question?"

Mark replied, "I'm sorry the presentation is not over so could you wait until it is please."

"I'm sorry to be rude, Dr Cooper, but my question is, could you get to the point as we have all been standing here for well over an hour already and so far we have heard nothing worth reporting on?"

"OK I will try to make this as brief as possible. While I can't say that we have discovered a cure for these illnesses, I can say we are on the brink of doing so, as we have discovered a new treatment that we believe will cure most of today's life threatening illnesses and at this moment we are looking to find enough volunteers to conduct clinical trials on. These trials will be conducted on 1500 patients who fit a precise criterion. The main requirement of this criterion is that we will only consider patients who have been diagnosed prior to today's announcement and the full extent of their condition is already known to their consultant or medical team. This treatment is still in its infancy and is still at least two years away from general use. However during these trials I believe we will achieve a large degree of success and if that is the case we will be carrying out additional trial's until the medical authorities register this treatment for general use, so don't be despondent or give up hope if you are not part of the first fifteen hundred. You can ask your questions now please."

The first question was.

"Dr Cooper, just how long have you been developing, this treatment?"

"I have been developing this treatment during the last 10 years and more."

"Why has it taken you this long to make any form of announcement? It seems strange to say the least; it's as if you have something to hide"

This guy was beginning to express his suspicion, which at first threw Mark off track but after a brief pause he re-composed himself.

"If you are so far along the way to finding this cure, why is this the first anyone has heard about it DR Cooper? Has this been kept secret due to the commercial interests of the pharmaceutical companies who have developed it?"

"First of all the pharmaceutical companies have no involvement in this treatment, it has been made possible by the commitment of the UK and US Governments.

We have not made this information public knowledge because we are still so far away from it being licensed for general use and we didn't want to make an announcement, prior to us being confident it will be licensed for use."

"After the first fifteen hundred, how will you select your next group?"

"In a similar manner to the way we will select the first fifteen hundred."

"So what type of cancer and other illnesses are we talking about being able to cure Dr Cooper?"

"I have to be cautious when I answer that question but during our lab tests on mice and other mammals, we have had success treating most types of cancers, brain disorders, mainly stroke, paralysis and many more ailments."

"How will this affect the current treatment provide by the pharmaceuticals?"

"I believe that once we can verify the treatment is as effective as we believe it will be. This treatment will replace all conventional treatment offered by these companies."

"Won't that cause these companies to close, with the loss of thousands of jobs?"

"We recognise that could be an issue but we have had to balance economy against people's health and well-being and in the mind of everyone involved with this discovery, health wins by a mile."

"That's easy for you to say as I'm sure you will become a very rich man as a result of this discovery and will still have a job to go to. So why would people's livelihood be something that would worry you?"

"I'm sorry but I find that statement to contemptuous to comment on. Thank you ladies and Gentlemen, the question session is now concluded."

Mark's speech was acknowledged with a rapturous fifteen minute ovation and cheers. Unfortunately it was also punctuated by a few boos, which were aimed at the journalist whose comments had caused the question session to end so abruptly.

The President announced.

"Members of the press before you send your copy off to your editors. The press officers would like to read them, so we are sure the facts, are being reported as they should be."

Matthew thought *even at this stage the Government are still censoring this information.*

Owing to the time for questions ending so abruptly, due to the idiot who had said what he had, the remainder of the press was vying for his blood and this was noticed by the President and so to prevent murder being committed. He decided to re-open the question session.

"Members of the press, I will allow a brief amount of additional time for more questions. However they must be relevant to the treatment, or I will end the session without further warning."

"Thank you Mr President, may I ask Dr Cooper a question?"

"Of course go ahead."

It was the same journalist who spoke first, " Dr Cooper I would like to apologise for being so rude by making the statement I did but this announcement seems to be hiding something and all I was trying to understand is what that may be?"

Mark responded by saying, "Yes we are trying to hide something."

The President couldn't believe that Mark was about to announce the suppression of miracle and braced himself for all the questions and criticism he would receive.

Mark continued, "But it is only like all inventions and discoveries, we want to keep under wraps how we made the discovery and what the treatment consists of."

The President breathed a sigh of relief.

If you're, so confident Dr Cooper, that your cure can already do what you claim, why do you need to conduct these trials?"

He continued, "Also why haven't you already made enough of the medicine during the last 10 years to use it on more than 1500 people?"

"I think I can answer both questions at the same time, without going into too much detail about the treatment, the serum is not a manmade drug, it's a donation from other people and just as with every other donation, be it blood, organ's, or even fertility donations, there have been a number of ethical issues we have had to consider prior to using this treatment."

"So why haven't we seen any advertising campaigns for potential donors?"

"That is because all campaigns have so far been carried out in Hospitals, on individuals who are able to be considered as a donor."

"Are you saying not everyone can donate?"

"That's right I am."

"So why's that Dr Cooper?"

Mark had to think quick and come up with an answer that would sound feasible.

"If you think about any donation, if the donor and the recipient don't match, the donation is rejected."

"So how do you intend to gather more of the serum?"

"As we speak, serum is being harvested in every hospital throughout the US and the UK" He continued, "Also as the trials progress we will be able to harvest more serum from every hospital worldwide."

"So why isn't that happening already?"

"We need to fully assess the effectiveness of the treatment before we commit that much resource to it." He continued, "Plus I will have to select a team of specialists to work with me who will need to know how to harvest and then administer the treatment."

"You said you were confident it will work so, why is that not happening today?"

"I am completely confident that it will work but unfortunately there are procedures that have to be followed before the whole of the medical establishment will accept it for general use and as I have already said, there are medical teams who are harvesting the serum as we speak."

"Thank you Dr Cooper."

"If there are no more questions I would like to bring to an end tonight's press release."

"Just two more Dr Cooper if you don't mind?"

"As long as there, relevant to the treatment itself go ahead."

"The first question Dr Cooper is, are there any side effects to the treatment?"

"There are no side effects what so ever."

"Could I ask the President the next question please, Dr Cooper?"

It was Peterson who replied, "Yes go ahead."

"Mr President would you call this a US or a UK breakthrough?"

"Ladies and Gentlemen it's neither, it's a joint collaboration by both governments on behalf of mankind as a whole and neither government would have been successful without the other."

The UK PM was asked if he would like to comment.

He began by acknowledging Mark's hard work.

"I think we should all recognise the debt we owe to Dr Cooper for this breakthrough. I've heard it described as the greatest breakthrough in medicine since penicillin."

The questioner continued.

"Mr President that brings me to one further question if you don't mind, will it replace penicillin?"

"Dr Cooper, could you answer that question please?"

"Yes of course Mr President. The simple answer to that is, no it won't replace penicillin or any current antibiotics. It will not be effective in curing epidemics or viral infections, conventional treatment will continue to be used to fight those."

The President announced. "Thank you the press conference is over."

The President took Mark to one side and thanked him for the recognition he gave too the two Governments. He also congratulated him on how he answered some of the awkward questions without giving anything away and that he felt sure he would be facing him in the political arena one day.

Mark said, "Somehow, I don't think so!"

Chapter 13
Ironic or What

It was the day of the Super Bowl and on this day nothing normally moves in the USA while the game is on and if you had not been lucky enough to have a ticket for the game. It was likely you and a group of buddies would be sitting in front of a TV in someone's house. The refrigerator full of Becks, Coors, Budweiser or any other cans of beer you could lay your hands on and in the kitchen at least one cupboard would be stocked with Pretzels, potato chips, nuts, lots of snacks to eat, while watching the game.

Interrupt this American institution at your peril.

Just like the FA Cup Final in England, the coverage started hours before the game began, it would take a lot for the TV broadcaster to interrupt this coverage but today a couple of hours before the game began, the build up to the game was interrupted with a News Flash.

We have breaking news that the Director General of the US Federal Medical Board, professor Andrew Armstrong has been found dead in a Washington police cell this morning. Police have confirmed professor Armstrong had been helping them investigate allegations into fraud and gross misconduct. Involving, the Federal Medical Board and the US Government. His wife is being comforted by her family and friends at her home in Beverly Hills, the news flash didn't seem to have much impact on most of the millions of TV viewers, their main concern was the coverage of the game being interrupted and how their team would perform on the day, football was more important than some unknown doctor. Once the game was over and The Seahawks had triumphed over the Broncos, a news update was broadcast by a film crew outside professor Armstrong's Beverly Hill's mansion, the commentator announced that professor Armstrong's body was found at 6.20 a.m. by police as they entered his cell with his breakfast, it is alleged professor Armstrong had taken his own life.

His wife said, "That for some reason my husband had seemed to be under greater stress these last few days, than I have ever seen him before."

A police spokesman said. "All the evidence, points to the professor taking his own life but no official announcement would be made into the cause of death until after an inquest had been conducted. Colleagues we have spoken to have stated that it was completely out of character for him to take his own life but added these last few days, professor Armstrong had been involved in some sort of judicial enquiry."

Back in Manchester the phone rang and Matthew picked up the receiver it was Mark.

"Mark where are you?" asked Matthew.

"I'm in London, you've got to get down here right away, the PM has been in touch, were leaving for Washington as soon as you arrive."

"OK I will check with the airport, to see when I can get a flight."

"No need you're being picked up in half an hour and taken to the airport your flight has already been arranged."

"Must be big whatever it is!"

Matthew no longer feared for his life, he trusted the PM simply because he was now working with the President.

Casting his mind back to his last trip to London, Matthew made sure he was dressed appropriately. He packed a medium sized suit case and picked up his lap top and on arrival at Manchester airport he was rushed through to the Executive VIP lounge, when he entered the waiter recognised him and asked him. "Could I get you a jug of Manhattan?"

"Yes please." He sat down lit a cigarette and helped himself to a glass.

"Would you like some snacks, Mr Michellin?"

Mathew was impressed the waiter, had remembered his name.

Before he could reply, he was told he needed to board the flight straight away, as he walked onto the aircraft he was delighted to be welcomed aboard by a familiar friendly face.

"Good afternoon, sir, it's a pleasure to welcome you aboard again."

"The pleasure's all mine, Karen," he replied, annoyed at himself that he could still remember her name.

"When you're comfortable in your seat sir, how about I mix you a jug of Manhattan?"

"Yes that's fine and how about you bring two glasses, so you can join me and we can get to know each other better, as it seems I may be using this service quite a lot in the future."

"I would love to, sir, but I'm not allowed, it's against company policy."

Come on, Karen, I'm sure the rules can be broken for a frequent flier like me?"

"Maybe just a fruit juice then, sir."

"OK that's fine by me."

"I'm sorry I have to take drinks up to the flight deck, I won't be long."

"Good is it the same pilot, as the other time?"

"Yes it is."

"I wonder if you could tell him I'm on board and I said hello."

"Yes of course I can."

She said "hello," to Matthew again.

"That was quick," he said.

"All I had to do was pass them their drinks, as they were busy with the flight plan, so I didn't hang around."

"I'm glad to hear that."

"Would you like another jug of Manhattan, sir?"

"Yes please but no more of the, sir."

"I don't know your name, so how else can I refer to you?"

"I'm called Matthew."

"That's a coincidence that was the name of my last boyfriend."

"Your last boyfriend, so does that mean I could be your next?"

"That's up to you isn't it."

"What do you mean by that?"

"I mean if you give me a ring, next time you're in Manchester, you could be."

"I can't if I don't have your number."

"I will give it to you when I return with the drinks."

"Hello there, Matthew, it's good to have you on board again,"

"Hello Captain Wilson."

"You seem deep in thought Matthew, should I leave you for a moment?"

"No you're not disturbing me."

"Problems, Matthew?"

"No I was just day dreaming, I had a lovely picture in my head, you see I'm hoping to bump into a friend when I reach Washington tonight."

"I don't think so, Mathew, by the time you arrive there, it will be long past tonight."

"Oh shit, it will won't it, so I'll just have to see if I can make alternative arrangements then, as the night is still young at least on this side of the pond, so I may just have to make a phone call when we touch down in London."

"Karen are you alright?"

"Yes thank you, Captain, I'm just taking a drink to our new frequent flier."

"Look after him Karen, he's a very important person."

"I will captain."

"Our guest is flying with the Prime Minister to the White house tonight, for an urgent meeting with the President."

"My, he is important isn't, he."

"Here is your drink Matthew and more important my number but I'm not sure I should call you Matthew."

"Why's that then?"

"I've just been told you're a very, very important person, so important that you're flying to meet the President tonight."

"That's right I am. Although I'm not really that important."

"What is it you do?"

"I'm sorry but I can't tell you."

"Why are you a spy?"

"Yes I am but don't tell anyone."

"Wow I've got my very own James Bond."

She continued, "Should I be Money Penny?"

Matthew replied, "I'd rather that to you being Q."

"Wow role playing already," she said.

On landing Matthew assured Karen he would phone her when he gets back into Manchester. He suggested they meet in Northern sector, a fairly new area of the town centre with lots of trendy bars and restaurants. Matthew was rushed directly to his flight to Washington with no time to make a phone call, he was lead to the first class lounge upstairs on the aircraft which had been fully reserved for the party, he said, "Hello" to each of them and attracted the attention of the pretty stewardess and invited her to meet him later for a drink when they arrived in Washington.

She said, "Let me think about it, sir."

Mark said, "Matthew do you never give it a rest?"

"Hang on I've been shown how short life is, I've been right to the edge and thankfully didn't go over it, there are lots of women in the world I've still to meet before I do eventually pop my clogs."

"I take it you don't believe in monogamy then Matthew?"

"Of course I do, I have a table made from it in my dining room at home."

"No, you Jerk, monogamy' not Mahogany."

"I don't think I've ever heard the word. Let me look it up in my dictionary."

He found the word and read it to himself.

Monogamy being faithful to one woman.

"Look, Mark, I've been there, done that, for over 30 years, you see the bar has been set so high and I haven't found anyone yet who can get close to it let alone over it, so I continue looking and fingers crossed, I may find what I'm looking for one day and until I do, I'm determined to bloody well enjoy myself."

"So, Matthew, what is it your looking for?"

"I don't know until I find it."

Matthew then asked Mark, "Do you believe in love at first sight Mark?"

"No I don't."

"Go on tell me why not?"

"I think that it's just a load of crap that has been created by Hollywood to sell films, that's why."

"That's the most cynical I've ever known you to be Mark."

"Do you believe in it then Matthew?"

"Without a doubt yes I do."

"Why's that Matthew?"

"That's because I've experienced it."

"What with your wife I take it?"

"Yes that's right it was."

"So how did you know?"

"I just did from the very first moment I met her, I can't explain it, but as mushy as this sounds if it happens, you somehow know it."

"I'm sorry, Matthew, to doubt you, but I still think its bull shit."

"So what's all this rushing to Washington about then?"

"Have you not seen the news today?"

"No I've not, what's happened?"

"Armstrong's committed suicide."

"Bullshit you're kidding."

"No I'm not, it's true."

"That can't be the only reason, not with all the miracle team here. Have you asked the PM what it's about?"

"Yes but he's not giving anything away."

On arrival in Washington they were met at the airport and rushed directly to the White House, the President was in the Oval office awaiting their arrival, "Welcome gentlemen, I'm sorry to rush you here tonight. So if we can get straight to the point, I have had some really bad news today."

Matthew said, "Do you mean about professor Armstrong?"

"No something much more personal than that. The first Lady and I have been informed that our youngest son has been diagnosed with being in the late stages of Leukaemia and we are hoping your treatment Dr Cooper will be able to help him."

"I don't know about that, sir, as that would go against everything we agreed. So I'm sorry, sir, I will have to consult the team to see what they think."

"OK Doctor Cooper but how soon can you do that?"

"As soon as you can get the team together, I can meet them."

"Good I'll get them together tomorrow morning will that be OK with the pair of you?"

"Yes of course, sir."

After this brief conversation the President left the room.

Mark said to Matthew, I don't like this Matthew. We all agreed that we stick to the original criteria and not swap and change due to privilege or include anyone who hadn't already been diagnosed prior to the press release and I bet the rest won't be happy either."

"Look Mark we said that top of the list would be children under twelve years of age, so if we would have known about his illness before the press release, would he have been on the list?"

"Yes of course he would."

"So Mark, what's the problem?"

"You know what the problem is; it's getting the others to go back on what we originally agreed."

"Fuck the others, Mark. It's your treatment, so as I see it, it's your call."

"OK, Matt, but It's not going to be easy to get them to agree. As very few of them have any time for Peterson."

"I know but let's try anyway and it's not Peterson it's his young son."

The following morning at the meeting, Mark spoke to the group and explained the situation and the request of the President and after a brief discussion by the group, who were anything but sympathetic to the President's request. It was Judge Lucy who said.

"Look Dr Cooper you know we discussed the possibility of something like this happening, that some VIP could try to make a case for themselves, or a connection of theirs to be allowed to gate crash the list at the expense of some ordinary person and that would be totally unfair. That's why we insisted that no one would be allowed to be added to the list if they were not aware of their condition prior to the press release and this is just the sort of thing we agreed we would not let happen no matter who they were. So as far as I'm concerned I'm not giving my approval."

"Look this is a young boy and the son of your President."

"Exactly that's what he is but that doesn't entitle him to receive special treatment and with respect would we be having this discussion if he was the son of the White house window cleaner?"

"I don't know would we?"

"No you know we wouldn't Dr Cooper and where will this end, what if next week his other son contracts an incurable illness, or his wife, or the son of the UK's PM falls seriously ill, where will it end? Are we prepared to compile a list just full of VIPs and their families and go back on everything we agreed and let the common man down, just for an incompetent President?"

"I'm sorry your Honour but I think you're being a little bit over dramatic and a bit too personal for my liking," interrupted Matthew, he then continued, "also what about your so called sense of justice and the morality of allowing a young boy to die just because of your feelings towards another human being?"

"I'm sorry but I don't think I am, so my decision remains the same, I'm not approving it and you're the last person I will be lectured by about morals Mr Michellin, so that's it, it's not happening."

"Now hang on, your accusing the President of making a unilateral decision to place his son on the list but isn't that what you're doing by saying you're not approving it," Matthew protested, "and let me remind you, it's not just up to you, there are more people in this room who have a say in this decision than you."

"That's right. So let's ask them shall we?"

The Judge asked everyone in the room to raise their arms if they were in favour of adding the boy to the list. The only hands to be raised was the hands of Matthew, Mark, and Monsignor O'Donnell, the Judge asked is that everyone? Which it was.

"Mr Michellin it would seem the answer is we won't allow him to be treated."

"OK gentlemen, so be it, we will tell the President of the decision." Matthew said "but before we do can I ask you to reconsider?"

"Sorry Mr Michellin the decision is final."

"OK but before we do tell him I want it known for the record that Mark, me and the Monsignor were in favour of treating the boy."

Matthew and Mark were sat in the dining room of the Willard hotel, awaiting the arrival of the President and when he arrived with his entourage of security staff he approached the pair of them.

Mark said "I'm sorry Mr President but I have bad news, we couldn't get them to agree to treat your son."

"So where does that leave us?"

"We have no option other than to rely on conventional treatment, sir," replied Mark.

The President's next comment was directed towards Matthew.

"I have to say Mr Michelin you disappoint me. I wouldn't have thought that even you would seek vengeance on my son by refusing him a chance to survive."

Matthew kept looking at the table and gave no reply.

The President continued by adding, "Dr Cooper I thank you for your attempt at trying to get my son added to the list." Ignoring Matthew completely and this really pissed Matthew off. Matthew thought to himself, *I'll make you pay for that one day Peterson.*

"Gentlemen I would like you to reconvene your meeting in the White house tomorrow at 9 a.m. where you will be joined by the rest of the judicial enquiry members and I myself will be in attendance throughout your discussions."

Once they left the hotel Matthew said to Mark, "I can't believe what he just said to me, when it was me who batted for him more than anyone."

"I know but don't let it get to you," replied Mark.

"He's going to pay for that comment."

"In what way" asked Mark?

"Well I'm going to be charging, quite a few hookers to the white house account tonight."

Both of them started to laugh.

Chapter 14
Cometh the Wrong Decision Cometh the Dictator

At 9 a.m. the following morning the team was sat together in the Map room and when the President entered he said, "Good morning gentlemen and thank you for attending at such short notice. You are all aware no doubt of the seriousness of my son's condition. I would like to ensure I understood the feedback which I received from Dr Cooper and Mr Michellin, following your meeting to discuss my son's condition, at which I believe it was decided that he would not be given the Miracle treatment and just be administered conventional treatment."

Everyone sat in total silence and couldn't even look in the direction of the President that is everyone other than Matthew, Mark and Monsignor O'Donnell, it was Matthew who said.

"Excuse me Mr President if I may just say something?"

"Of course you may Mr Michellin, as long as it's relevant."

Matthew said "come on you all had enough to say yesterday, when no one would be able to point a finger at any of you and blame you but now you have to look the President in the eye you're just like frightened little children scared of being told off for something you have done wrong. You're nothing but a set of fucking coward's, I'm sorry for my language sir."

The President looked at Matthew and thought *I think I may have misjudged you, Mr Michellin.*

"May, I carry on, sir?"

"Yes, go ahead, Matthew."

"Mr President as it's now 10:30 a.m., may I respectfully request we take a natural break and we reconvene in 30 minutes to resume our discussion in your absence?"

"Very well gentlemen we will do that. Mr Michellin when would you suggest I re-enter the meeting?"

"I would suggest that if you could allow us a further 60 minutes alone sir?"

"Very well then gentlemen I will re-enter the meeting at12 noon."

Both Judge's Lucy and Melvin cornered Matthew and asked him what the hell did he think he was playing at?

Matthew replied, "I'm not playing at anything I'm just trying to bring about some justice here."

"How do you see this as Justice Mr Michellin, by you trying to overrule the rest of us?"

"I'm not trying to overrule any one I'm just asking you to reconsider your decision."

"No you're not, what your doing is trying to bully and put pressure on us in front of the President so you can win his pathetic approval," said Lucy.

"Can't you understand I'm trying to save a young boys life here."

"What I understand, Mr Michellin, is that whatever you say you won't get me to change my mind and I'm prepared to let nature take its course with this boy, so for me he has no more right to live than any other youngster."

"You know you really are a piece of fucking shit aren't you, Lucy." Matthew continued, "Go on Melvin, fine me now you incompetent prick."

"Well Mr Michellin you have just lived up to my opinion of you I expressed it in court the other day."

"Fuck off, Melvin, just who the fuck do you think you are?"

"I'm a high court Judge that's who I am."

"Not out here you're not, out here you're just a fucking little man who uses big words that's all you are."

Melvin went on to say, "Mr Michellin, we all took a vote yesterday and we all agreed that the boy wouldn't be added to the list because he didn't fit the original criteria that we instructed the press we would use to pick the first 1500 and that is he wasn't aware of his condition prior to the announcement taking place."

"I didn't agree, nor did Mark, or the Monsignor."

Lucy now entered the conversation, "That's right you didn't but the majority did and this being a democracy our vote won so accept it." He carried on, "At the start of this we said we wouldn't add anyone to the list especially if they weren't aware of their illness prior to the press announcement."

Matthew replied, "I know what we said but we also said we would be compassionate."

Lucy continued, "But we insisted that celebrity wouldn't make us change our minds and now just because we have the President's son falling ill, you three want us to change the rules just so you can impress the President."

"It's nothing to do with impressing the President."

Matthew continued, "We originally agreed that at the top of the list, would be children under the age of 12 years old and that fit's this young boy, so you're saying just because of time scale you are condemning the boy to die."

"You're stretching it now, Mr Michellin."

"How the fuck can I be stretching it, you are condemning the boy to death."

Nasty Matthew now surfaced. "What's up, Lucy, are you missing getting your kicks since the death penalty was abolished and you can now get yourself off with this kid?"

"Michellin that is the most offensive thing I have ever heard, I want you to apologise to me now."

"I wouldn't hold my breath if I was you."

Lucy said, "You're nothing but an English yob Michellin and if you call it justice by allowing him to be added to the list, what about the injustice of him taking someone's place on it?"

Melvin now wanted his say on the issue, "So how does your justice help them, Michellin?"

"They will be the very first name to be added to the second list."

"That doesn't seem like justice to me, just an excuse for adding the President's son."

Matthew said, "If we can't look after our own families who can we look after?"

Back in the meeting Matthew put the very same argument to the other members, however none of them agreed, saying it was just a reason for adding the boy to the list.

Mark said, "OK well consider this scenario will you. How just is this then, a young family regardless of status or connection, sit down and watch a TV broadcast that announces a miracle cure is in the development stage and that 1500 people will be given the chance to be saved by this treatment. Then imagine their horror when they discover shortly afterwards that their son has a terminal illness, neither of them can believe what's happening and neither can comfort the other, until one of them remembers the announcement of miracle, suddenly they are full of hope thinking that their son has a chance of recovering, neither sleep a wink that night, determined that first thing the very next morning they will contact their child's specialist, who tells them their child cannot be considered for treatment just because he was diagnosed to late, even though he may well have had the condition before the announcement, so this youngster who has their whole life ahead of them is condemned to death. Yet some 65 year old is considered for treatment in their place, even though they have lived a long and fulfilled life and you are prepared to add another 20 something years to their life. Just because of a time limit, regardless of whom the child maybe, this decision has to be wrong."

Matthew couldn't sit in silence any longer and said, "So if you're adamant about continuing with your original decision so be it but it's you who will inform the President when he re -enters the room not me nor DR Cooper."

The President re- entered the room. The atmosphere was tense. Matthew spoke up saying, "Mr President, we have gone over yesterday's decision and arrived at our conclusion and I believe that Judge Lucy would like to inform you of the decision."

"Go ahead then, Graham, would you like to tell me what the decision is about treating my son?"

"Yes, sir, I would but as the spokesman for the group, I am really just the messenger and sadly I have to announce on behalf of everyone, that when we agreed to the criteria for a list of trialists we stated that the list must be drawn up from people who were aware of their illness prior to the announcement to the press and that under no circumstances would anyone be considered for the trials who had not already been diagnosed, regardless of who that person maybe, sir, even if it was yourself, the Queen of England or anyone else."

"So what does that mean, Graham?"

"It means, that we have confirmed our decision stands and the boy will not be added to the list."

"Yes I recall that decision gentlemen but let me remind you all, I am the President of the United States of America and without my decision to allow this treatment to go ahead nobody would be on the list."

"Yes we do appreciate that, sir."

"Good it's time for you to appreciate this as well, I'm the President of the USA and I'm advising you that your decision has been over ruled and you will make the treatment available to this child."

The President allowed himself to have a quick glance around the table at the faces of everyone, when he looked at Matthew he was surprised to see a triumphant smirk on his face.

The President said, "Dr Cooper, Mr Michellin, and Monsignor O'Donnell, if you have time I would like to have a private word with the three of you in my study."

"Yes of course, sir," they all replied.

The President began to leave the room and on his way out, he turned around and said to the remaining members of the group, who were still in the room.

"I would like to thank you all for your time and assistance with this issue and gentlemen I can assure you all, I will never forget what you have done today."

The group looked at one another and started to mumble words of regret.

Jonathan Smalling said, "That sounded like a threat to me," others were saying, I told you that we should have allowed the treatment to go ahead, he's obviously going to look for revenge, they all sat there like scared little children. Graham piped up and said. "Don't worry about him, what harm, can he do to us?"

Melvin said, "That's right, with the upcoming elections, he will more than likely be voted out of office, so in six months we will probably have a new Republican President."

"Six months a long time though," Kevin said.

The President entered his study sat down breathed a sigh of relief and lit himself a cigar, he then spoke to a servant by the internal telephone and asked them to prepare a large jug of Manhattan and bring it along with four glasses to his study as soon as it's ready.

There was immediately a knock on the door and the President asked them to enter.

"Sit down gentlemen. Do you mind if I finish my cigar?"

Mark said "Not at all, sir, carry on."

"Would you like one yourselves?" he asked them.

They all replied, "Yes thank you, sir, we would." The President opened the box of cigars and offered one to each of them. He thanked them for their help today.

"Don't mention it, sir," replied Matthew.

"So gentlemen can I also tempt you with a glass of your favourite tipple?"

Matthew said "and what would that be, sir?"

"Now come on Matthew that would be a Manhattan."

"Yes please, sir."

The President then said, "I'm sorry Matthew that I can't provide you with a woman as well, political correctness and all that and I'm sure the Monsignor would have something to say if I did."

Matthew replied, "Yes he'd probably ask for one himself," they all laughed.

Matthew then said, "Not to worry, sir, two out of three ain't bad."

The President said, "Could be a good title for a song that."

A servant shortly afterwards entered the study carrying a tray containing a large jug and four glasses.

"So, Dr Cooper, can I fully depend on you to help my child?"

"Yes of course you can, sir."

"Thank you, Dr Cooper, and what would be the earliest we could start the treatment?"

"First of all, sir, I would have to travel to my clinic and return with the serum."

Matthew interrupted, "Can I suggest to save time wouldn't it be better to take the patient with you and treat him there."

"Yes it would be but would the President allow that to happen?"

"Dr Cooper, seeing as though we are now working together and no longer need to keep secretes from each other, I think you would have to tell me where that was and you would have to be prepared to be accompanied by secret service personnel."

"That's fine by me, sir, It's not like you're going to shut me down any longer is it."

"That's right Dr Cooper it's not. So where is your clinic?"

"It's, on ST Kitts, sir."

"Very nice," the President replied "you've not exactly been slumming it then have you, Mark?"

"No but there have been times when It's not been as good as It's cracked up to be."

"Whys that, Mark?"

"There was one day a couple of weeks ago, when my house keeper couldn't get me some bourbon."

"My God man, how did you cope?"

"It was hard, sir, as I had to suffer with Gin and Tonic instead."

"Disgraceful," replied the President.

"Matthew may I have a moment of your time in private?"

"Of course, sir, how can I help you?"

They both left the room.

"I would like to offer my sincere apologies, for my behaviour yesterday and by jumping to the wrong concussion by accusing you of preventing my son from being treated. I could tell by your behaviour and your attitude in the meeting today plus your expression when I over ruled the decision that you were and always had been in favour of treating my son."

"That's alright, sir but you don't have to apologise, I realise how upset you were."

"Thank you and Dr Cooper once again and I can't thank either of you enough."

"It's not a problem, sir, we were both just trying to do the right thing, far too many people have suffered and are still doing so."

"However, Matthew, I do have a couple of favours to ask of you and I presume the first one will be you and not Dr Cooper of who I need to ask this favour of?"

"What's that, sir?"

"Matthew, could you stop charging hookers to the White house account."

"Of course, sir but could I ask you why would you presume It's me and not Mark?"

"Come on Matthew who else would it be?"

"OK fair point, sir."

"May I thank you once again on behalf of the first lady and me?"

"Don't mention it, sir."

"Anyhow Matthew I will have to leave now and give the first lady the good news but before I do, I would like to invite you and your good lady to have dinner with me and the first lady, at the White house, when you return from treating my son."

"I would be delighted to accept, sir."

"That's good and what should I tell the first lady that your good lady is called?"

"Would you excuse me for a moment, sir, I just have to check something with Mark?"

"Yes that's fine."

"Thank you, sir, I will be back in a second."

"Once back inside the room Matthew said to Mark, hey Mark what's she called again?"

"What's who called?"

"My Russian beauty that's, who?"

"You mean Ekaterina?"

"That's it."

He went back outside to the President, "sorry about that, sir."

"That's OK, Matthew."

"My girlfriend's name is Ekaterina."

"That's a nice but also an unusual name."

"It's Russian, sir."

The President now feeling much better since he knew his son was to be treated; he joked with Matthew and said "She's not a spy is she?"

"I wouldn't have thought so."

The President said, "If she is a spy, I'm sure when we check out her background it will come to light. So if you could provide us with all her details, you know the type of thing, surname, date of birth, that type of thing."

Matthew began to feel his eyes glaze over and he thought to himself, *it looks like It's going to be a burger at MacDonald's with some White house gardener then. This is going to be embarrassing when I ask Mark to get the details for me.* The meeting between President Peterson, Mark, Matthew, and the Monsignor, reconvened.

The President asked Mark, "Are you still confident that your treatment will cure my son, Dr Cooper?"

"Yes I am, sir, as ever."

"Thank you, Dr Cooper, I'll be forever in your debt."

The President thanked them all once again and said, "I must go now to give the first lady the good news."

The rest of the members of the committee gathered together and it was Graham who spoke first and said, "I don't know about the rest of you but I feel totally humiliated by what Peterson has just done in there and I'm telling you, there is no way I'm letting him get away with it. He needs to be stopped he's nothing more than a dictator. We can't allow him to be re-elected."

"I know but how can we stop him?" replied Steven.

Graham said "I don't know but I'm going to find a way of doing so."

Graham gave them all an invitation, "Can I ask you all to join me for lunch next Friday at my chambers and we can discuss the matter then."

That would be good thank you, they all agreed.

"Gentlemen, I'm due back in court this afternoon, so I'm afraid I will have to leave you all for now."

Chapter 15
Let's Get this Show on the Road

Mark and Matthew returned to the bar of the Willard hotel, where they immediately started work on the list. They both opened their laptops and accessed their emails to find information of patients from all of the hospitals in the US and the UK, who were being recommended for the trials. They both had at the top of their list the son of the President. Matthew was still looking through his email to find his second name, he started to list all the names of the children under 12 years old and he then began to list the pregnant women, following that with the parents of children under 12 years old, he eventually ended up with a list of about 400 names.

Whereas Mark had no trouble finding his second name, it was Matthew Michellin however he was still looking at the children on the list and he ordered another pitcher of Manhattan, when it was brought to the table and the waitress left. They started to compare names on each other's list. Mathew was surprised to see his name so high on Mark's list and started to protest. Mark was having none of it saying. "Without you Matthew we wouldn't be where we are today and besides I made you a promises and I intend to stick by it. You will be taking a second trip on Air Force One. You're flying with me and the President's son to my clinic and I'm going to treat both of you at the same time. So with a bit of luck, in a month or so, Matthew, you may well be chasing that Goddess of yours around the bed room."

"I hope not," replied Matthew, "I don't even have to do that now, so if that's what your treatment will do causing women to run away from me, you can stick your dammed serum up your ass."

Chapter 16

Back on the Island

The flight to St Kitts took off, with the two patients on board, including Mark and four secret service personnel. Once they had arrived at the clinic, all the usual medical checks were carried out and there was a nice bonus for Matthew, the nurse tending to him was the receptionist from the hotel he had previously stayed at with Ekaterina, he thought to himself life's already getting better, this time he asked her what she was called.

She replied. "My name is Linda."

He then said, "I have such a poor memory for names, could you write it down for me because I'm sure I will forget it before I leave the island," and he was determined that he would.

His treatment was scheduled for 1 p.m. the next day. He was told he would be spending the night in the clinic and was under strict instruction that he must not have any alcohol until after his treatment.

The following day the treatment was carried out on both patients it was a small painless procedure that just required an injection of the serum into the spinal cord. Matthew let out a loud yell, whereas the child made no noise what so ever, in addition to the treatment the boy was still having chemotherapy during his time in the clinic, "That's it, Matthew, all done, now we just need to monitor your progress over the next four weeks."

Four weeks later Matthew was already showing signs of recovery, first of all his peripheral vision in his left eye started to improve and he could start to move his fingers and toes, he still had trouble using his hand or arm in any worthwhile way, however during the four weeks he felt some kind of improvement each day and he couldn't wait to wake up each morning just to see what else he was able to do, he noticed a slight tingling in his limbs every day, it felt like he was having tiny electric shocks in his left side limbs, it was a strange feeling, rather than it being painful to be honest he found it quite exhilarating. He had been so determined to get better, he had even taken the pledge not to consume any alcohol during the four weeks and while each day he improved somewhat, it was now killing him that he hadn't had a drink for so long, the improvements in the boy were not as obvious, as he was fully mobile before the treatment but the good news was his test results were positive and his leukaemia was in remission.

When it came to the end of the course of treatment and it was time to fly back to the States, Matthew still hadn't fully recovered as he still had very limited movement in his arm and his hand, although Mark was delighted with his progress, he was even able to walk without his walking stick completely unaided out of the clinic and to the car and because Air Force One was undergoing maintenance, he would have to stay in a hotel until Air Force One would arrive to fly them back to Washington, he climbed into the car, which was taking him to the hotel he had previously stayed at on his first visit. when he arrived at the hotel, he tracked down Linda and arranged to meet her for a drink that evening, he couldn't make his mind up what he was looking forward to most, either adding Linda to his list of conquests, or his first Manhattan, either way he knew he would do both that evening.

He was only due to stay at the hotel for three nights, until Air Force One was available to take them back to Washington but wow what a three night spell that had been, not only had he made up for and more, his four weeks of abstinence from alcohol, he had even met two ladies who had been visiting the island on business but don't ask him what they were called as he had no idea. While leaving the hotel on the morning of his flight, Linda the receptionist said, "It's been really nice spending some time with you, maybe we will see each other again one day?"

Matthew replied, "I will look forward to that."

She said "see you again then, Matthew."

He turned and said, "yes err see you again, err, err, yes see you again," no point in trying to remember her name, as he didn't have a clue and he thought to himself *that's fair enough, there's been two other names since her he couldn't remember.* As he walked out of the hotel she looked at him and thought *you bastard*!

Chapter 17

It's Good News Week

On the plane on the way home, Matthew seemed to be a bit down. Mark asked him "what's wrong, Matthew?"

He replied, "Oh nothing."

"Come on, Matthew, there's something not right, what is it?"

"I thought I would be able to use my hand and arm by now."

"Don't worry, Matthew, you will, just give it time, you've been living with your condition for so long, It's just that you may need another course of treatment that's all but it will work I promise. Just look at the progress you've already made so it proves it works; you'll be fine don't worry."

"I hope so."

"You will be, don't worry."

The three of them were taken directly to the White house where they were met by the President and Joanna, the first lady who immediately hugged her young son. The President remarked just how much of a difference there was with Matthew.

Then Mark said "I have some fantastic news, sir, the latest results show your sons in complete remission."

Peterson and his wife, hugged each other and both of them started to cry uncontrollably. "Mark we can't thank you enough."

"That's OK, sir, don't mention it."

"You must both join Joanna and me for dinner tonight and maybe we can find out something more about Ekaterina?"

Mark said, "I wouldn't bank on that, sir."

"None the less, we would like to have dinner, with the two of you this evening, say about 8 p.m.?"

"Yes, sir, that's fine gives us enough time to freshen up."

Mark said to Matthew, "Puts you in a bit of a dilemma tonight that doesn't it."

"Why, what do you mean?"

"It leaves you no time to work your magic on the girls in the hotel; by the time we get back there it will be too late, well past 12 p.m."

Matthew said, "Well there's no other way for it then, tonight it's going to have to be the midnight train to Georgia."

Mark asked "do you have a favourite type of woman, Matthew?"

To which he replied, "No I don't have a favourite type of woman, every woman is my type, just as long as I know her name before I've slept with her, after that it's anyone's guess."

He then asked Matthew, "Once you regain your mobility, what do you intend to do?"

"First of all, I've got six years of my life to make up for, I want to regain my driving licence, buy a nice car and do route 66 and also play golf again"

"What would you really like to do, if you could?"

"I have always wanted to fly in a jet fighter or a world war two bomber, either a Lancaster or a B52."

"Is that all? I'm sure that could be arranged."

"No I would love to visit the playboy grotto."

"Well that could be a bit more difficult."

"Look, Mark, I've met people of late, who I never imagined I would ever meet, so you never know I could still meet Heff one day."

"Keep fantasising, Matthew! Is that it now?"

"No I'm going to re-acquaint myself with a particular politician I met back in Manchester and thank him for all his help."

While all this was going on. Judge Graham Lucy was plotting with the others a way to stop Peterson being re-elected.